STOLEN TRINKETS

THE CHAOS MAGES BOOK I

ALEX STEELE

STEEL FOX MEDIA LLC

STOLEN TRINKETS

THE CHAOS MAGES BOOK I

ALEX STEELE

First edition, July 2018
Version 1.0, July 2018
***ISBN* 978-1-7324518-0-3**

Cover by Deranged Doctor Design
Character illustrations by Zhivko Zhelev

A big thank you to my ART (Advanced Reader Team) AKA Berserker Reader Team. They helped turn a good book into a great one.

Arielle Fragassi, Cassandra Hall, Chris Christman II, David B., David M., Denise King, Larry Diaz Tushman, Laura Rogers, Penny Campbell-Myhill, Rob Hill, Sue Watts, Tami Cowles, Terri Adkisson, Tom Ryan

To my proofreader Carol Rushing. You provided me with a clean draft to send to the ART team, thanks for the hard work.

Lastly, I want to thank Sarah Burton at An Avid Reader Editing. She, as well as a few members in the group, convinced me to restructure the first chapter of the book to make it more engaging. Your feedback is priceless.

From Alex:

Be grateful for today and never take anything for granted.

Waste not, want not.

Live every day as if it were your last.

From Stephanie:

Thank you, Alex, for trusting me to put words to your ideas.

This truly feels like **our** *story.*

CONTENTS

ONE

It had been a few weeks since someone had tried to kill me. These attempts always ended in failure for the assassins; I just ended up late for work and got chewed out for making a scene. You'd think they'd give up eventually.

I adjusted my grip on the handrail and glanced over my shoulder at the crowded commuter car. A Japanese man with a goatee was at my five o'clock. He hadn't looked at me directly since we boarded, but he was watching my reflection in the shiny chrome trim on the interior of the passenger car. They had no windows due to something about the sight of inter-dimensional travel burning your eyes from your skull and melting your brain out of your ears if you ever gazed upon it.

Next to Goatee – the nickname seemed fitting – was a twitchy man wearing a hoodie pulled down far enough that I couldn't see his face. Tattoos extended down onto his fingers and thumbs that spelled out MAGIC BITES. He seemed...well adjusted.

Straight ahead was a blonde-haired woman dressed casually in jeans, a t-shirt, and a tailored coat that hugged her curves. She kept her body angled away from me, but every couple of minutes she looked past me at the two men.

A short sword hung at her hip, but that wasn't unusual. Many supernaturals carried a weapon but we had an old-fashioned idea about honor. No one carried guns; it was all blood and blades with us.

I glanced at the map that showed our progress. We were less than two minutes away from the stop. The would-be assassins wouldn't attack me before we debarked the Rune Car and left the station itself. No one could pay an assassin enough for them to martyr themselves trying to kill you.

Moira was heavily policed and protected supernatural city, but the Rune Rail system went above and beyond. It was guarded by Valkyries – how they got the Valkyries remained a mystery. They lurked, sight unseen, until someone threw a punch. Or drew a blade. Or cast any spell meant to harm. A few people managed to survive their retribution for a few seconds, but most vanished into a pink mist faster than you could blink. No one delayed the Rune Rail. Ever.

Everyone swayed forward as the passenger car came to a gentle stop. A wave of magic passed through the crowd that made my skin crawl. It wasn't exactly painful, but it was uncomfortable, especially since no one knew how it worked.

I kept my eyes forward as the crowd spilled out onto the platform. In my periphery, I could see the woman following me. The two men were most likely following me as well, but I wasn't going to make it obvious that I had spotted them. Yet. Of course it was possible I was mistaken and they were just stalkers. I got those a lot too and, try as I might, it was pretty much impossible to stop that entirely.

Two large escalators led up to the main floors of the Rune Rail Station. Everyone who wanted to stand waited in a neat line on the right, leaving room to jog up on the left if you were in a hurry. I thought about making my potential stalkers wait in the line on the right-hand side with me, but I was already cutting it close to get to work on time. If I had to have a *conversation* with them, I was going to be very late.

I hurried up the left side of the escalator. The Rune Rail levels of Moira were always packed; it truly was the city that never slept. Since there was no real sky to see, a combination of runes and technology – runetech – were used to illuminate the ceilings. It cycled through simulations of the skies, changing hourly, and was currently showing a cloudy, but sunny, sky from who knew where.

Moira – the city between worlds – was what started the Magical Revolution, uniting supernaturals and prosaics after centuries of keeping our magic in the shadows. Moira was nowhere, and everywhere, at the same time. You couldn't find it on a map, but the Rune Rail connected it to every major city in the world. No one knew how it was created, or where the mysterious city *was*, but every supernatural wanted to be there.

It provided an oasis away from the prosaics – what mages called those without magical talents. Twenty minutes or less and the Rune Rail could take you to any major city in the world you wanted. All you needed was a little magic in your blood. Of course, that meant trouble could follow you just as fast.

I let the crowd sweep me along until I reached what was colloquially known as the Crossroads. It was the first floor above the Rune Rail and home to some of the busiest shops, leading to a sort of pedestrian traffic jam. I went right and followed one of the smaller roads away from the mess. If this was going to get violent, I needed to be as far away from the crowds as possible.

As I walked past a storefront lined with glass, I kept an eye on the reflection. Sure enough, they were still following me. With a sigh, I glanced at my watch again. I was definitely going to be late.

The roads on each level of Moira were laid out in a precise grid. The farther out you went, the quieter it got. Some of the less glamorous businesses found a home out here. There were also run down apartments that housed the people who worked in Moira but were not wealthy enough to afford condos on the upper levels.

The crowd thinned to a trickle, then became non-existent. My stalkers were very obvious at this point. Goatee stayed about five meters behind me, and Hoodie paced me on the other side of the street. The woman, however, had disappeared at some point. That meant she was probably the one to worry about.

The business just ahead had a sign plastered in the window saying it had been repossessed due to non-payment of rent. A few meters beyond the building, the street ended at what was called the Edge. Reaching the borders of Moira was like reaching the edge of the world. It just ended, fading into a hazy darkness. A force field powered by runetech kept anyone from falling off, but being this close always sent a chill up my spine; it was like looking into the Abyss. Businesses stuck near the Edge never did well.

Whatever happened next was probably going to be messy. This seemed like as good a place as any to minimize potential property damage. I had a bit of an issue with causing that.

I stopped mid-step and turned to face the two men.

"I don't suppose you just came to chat?" I asked, my tone hopeful. I liked to give mercenaries a chance to come to their senses. They never did, but it made me feel chivalrous.

Goatee frowned at my flippancy and took a step forward, cracking his knuckles. "You have given the boss enough trouble. Today it ends," he said in a deep, gravelly voice.

He could be talking about so many different people. I could ask which person he meant, but that normally just insulted them and was rather pointless.

"With just the two of you? Come on, last time they sent four." I grinned and rested my palm on the hilt of the katana hanging on my hip. The magic inside it rose to meet my own and I felt everything click into place. "We can wait for the lady to show up, but if you think that'll make me go easy on you, you're out of luck. I don't discriminate."

"I will enjoy the sound of your pleading right before I take your head," Goatee said. Without further monologuing, he rushed forward.

I drew my katana, the blade singing as I pulled it out of the sheath. The blade didn't glint in the light; the steel was pure black and seemed to devour the light rather than reflect it.

Goatee gestured, burning a rune right into the air. He thrust his hand against the blazing symbol, and a dagger of bright green light shot toward me. I cut through it, and the magic crackled around me as the spell broke and dissipated.

I pushed off the ground with my right foot, but a manhole cover pounded into my right arm and hip, slamming me into a wall five feet away. Several of the bricks crumbled from the impact of my shoulder, while I slumped to the asphalt. My kidney felt like…well, it felt like a fifty-pound manhole lid had just crushed it; and I was fairly certain it broke a rib or two. I would have to deal with the damage later.

The manhole cover slid away, sparking against the concrete. The woman stalked forward. Her coat was gone, and her long blonde hair waved around her as if she were floating underwater. That gave me an idea.

I traced a quick rune over the ground with my hand. The magic hovered in place, glowing bright orange. I wrapped my hand around the rune and, with a tight grip on my katana to keep from screwing it up, pumped it full of power. This was going to be fun.

TWO

The air around my hand vibrated from the energy I was pouring into the rune. Hoodie finally got tired of waiting and darted forward. He flicked his wrist and a smoky blade raced toward me. Time seemed to slow as I took in the three mages converging on me.

I always wondered what could compel someone to kill for money. Based on the hungry gleam in Goatee's eye as he sprinted toward me, I guessed money for him. His feet pounded against the pavement as he gestured in the air, summoning his magic.

The woman stayed back, her fingers dancing through the air. I heard the clang of something metal but didn't see the manhole cover until it was flying past Goatee, headed straight for my face. Jerking back, I released the rune.

For six meters all around us in a perfect sphere, gravity just stopped working.

I was expecting it, but it was still hard to keep from flipping upside down when I pushed off the ground to dodge the projectile. My back scraped against the rough brick of the building behind me, but I had to stay close to it or I'd risk floating off.

Goatee was moving forward with too much momentum to stop himself. The manhole cover had continued on its original trajectory, and, to my intense satisfaction, the two collided. It hit him square in the face, knocking a tooth out of his jaw. Blood bubbled out of his mouth, floating around in a wobbly sphere. I couldn't have timed that better if I'd tried.

As the manhole hit Goatee, Blondie was launched in the opposite direction from the force of the impact. Her back smacked against the glass window of the shop across the street, shattering it. She disappeared into the building with a shocked expression. I guess no gravity made her magic a bit weird to use.

Hoodie was floating upside down. His green eyes flashed and were the only things I could see in the shadows of his hood. I knew that look; he was the sort of guy who killed people, not for the money, but for the hell of it.

"You've got less than six seconds to surrender and walk away from all this," I shouted the offer down at them. I was still rising, and would until I bounced off something. Or until gravity came back, which it would be doing any second now.

Goatee spat another glob of blood from his mouth and raised his hand toward me. "You're gonna burn for this!" he shouted, baring his red-streaked teeth at me. At least, what was left of them.

Seven...Eight...

Purple flames erupted from his palm and twisted straight at me through the air. I kicked off the building behind me and flew over the magic.

Nine...Ten.

Gravity came back with a vengeance as I passed over Goatee. I held the katana with one hand and drove it down, straight into his leg. We hit the ground, and the blade stabbed through his thigh into the concrete.

He screamed in pain, his voice strangled from the crushing weight of doubled gravity. That was the fun part about this rune. Until I canceled it, gravity would end for ten seconds, then come back doubled. It was twice as strong this time, but with the next cycle, it would be three times as strong. I had never let it go past three cycles, and that was pushing it. Even as a mage, my body didn't do well in those conditions.

I kept up the mental count. The main advantage this spell gave me was knowing when it would shift again. I didn't want to be surprised along with them.

The sudden increase in gravity made my cracked ribs ache something fierce. I gritted my teeth and ripped the katana from his leg. He rolled to his side and clutched the injured limb.

Hoodie had landed on his head but was slowly pushing himself back onto his feet, leaving a smudge of blood on the asphalt. The tinkle of glass drew my attention.

Three...Four...

To my right, the shattered glass that was scattered on the street lifted like a glittering curtain. The blonde-haired woman stepped out of the empty window, a murderous expression on her face. Well...that wasn't good.

With an angry shriek, she sent the glass flying right at me. Maybe her motivation was actually just pent up rage. I lifted my katana and braced my hand against the back of the blade. I had to be careful, even while using my focus, not to overdo this.

Five...Six...

The glass streaked toward me, tinkling as it bounced together. I leaped toward it, and a wave of dark green magic poured out of my sword. It collided with the glass shards and consumed them. Dust rained onto the concrete below.

Seven...Eight...

I charged toward Hoodie and ducked as he slung

another summoned blade at me. I kicked him in the gut, then swept his legs. He hit the ground with a thud, and I stomped on his head, cracking it against the curb. He probably wasn't dead, but...eh...

Nine...Ten.

Gravity vanished. I kicked up, then launched myself off the building again. Blondie was a little more prepared this time, but launching the manhole cover at me again still pushed her back, slamming her against the concrete. Her skull bounced off the ground, but the impact didn't knock her out.

I grabbed the ledge of the broken window and forced myself to the ground near her feet. She kicked out, aiming for my knee. I jerked my leg out of reach of the strike and launched myself to her left, bringing my sword down in an arc. I stopped it less than an inch from her neck.

She froze. My toes lifted slightly off the ground, but I was slowly drifting upward. I pressed the cold metal edge of the katana to her throat, just to make sure I had her full attention.

"If you get offered this job again, remember that it's not worth the money."

“Go to hell –”

I flipped the blade over and brought the dull side down on her temple. That shut her up real fast.

With my left hand, I drew the rune needed to cancel

the gravity loop and dropped to the ground. Blondie fell in a heap, and I left her there. This was not my mess to clean up.

I flicked my blade sharply, and the blood coating it splattered onto the pavement. I knelt beside Goatee and wiped it clean on his shoulder. He groaned in pain, glaring at me with a mix of fear and rage. The wound was bad, but he was a mage. He'd heal the injury in a couple of days at most.

I stood and re-sheathed the katana, then texted one of the sergeants in my division. They'd know what I meant, I had to send these texts often enough.

Clean up on level 12, near Edge,
30th and Border St.

These particular assassins were second-rate. It was almost as if whoever sent them didn't actually want me dead. Shaking my head, I texted the individual I was fairly certain was responsible. It was almost always the same, persistent asshole.

If you miss me, you could just call
or send flowers. No need to send
assassins.

THREE

I strolled into my department twenty minutes late and headed toward my office, which was nothing more than a large desk in a small room with no door. Most detectives shared an office with their partner, but I was fortunate enough to work alone.

IMIB, the International Magical Investigations Bureau, was located in Moira. It was run by a cooperative council made up of the Mage's Guild and representatives of the other supernatural races. The IMIB offices were on the thirty-second level – a few floors below the swanky, over-priced condos where the rich and powerful lived – but above the Rune Rail, busy stores, and the entertainment district.

"Blackwell," Chief Bradley shouted, stepping out of his office with a thick red folder in his hand. His name was fitting since I was almost certain the tank was named after him. He was stocky and wide, though not all of his bulk was muscle these days.

Standing in front of him was possibly the most beautiful woman I had ever seen, and perhaps the most eccentric. A blood-red trench coat hung down to the top of her knee-high leather boots – but that wasn't the eccentric part. She had bright pink hair that hung around her face in a sleek bob. Her eyes were the same color, though a deeper shade that bordered on purple.

"Yes, sir?" I asked, pausing in the walkway. If he knew about the fight, I was about to get chewed out. Probably in front of the whole department.

"Why are you late?" Bradley asked, his mustache bristling in expectation of needing to yell at me.

"Slept through my alarm clock," I lied with a smile. The less he knew, the better. There wasn't any serious damage this time anyhow.

"I want to talk to you in my office in ten minutes. Don't *sleep through your alarm* on the way here," Bradley snarked, obviously suspicious of my weak excuse, before heaving his bulk through the door.

The pink-haired beauty barely looked at me before following him inside. I, however, couldn't tear my eyes away from her.

Hot coffee splashed against my chest and I jumped

back with a yelp. My recently healed ribs twinged as the hot liquid stung my chest.

"Dammit, Blackwell, watch where you're going," Peterson snapped. Coffee dripped from his chin and the file he was holding.

"I wasn't the one walking," I muttered, pulling my soaked shirt away from my skin. I'd have to get that stain out; I didn't want to have to send yet another suit to my dry cleaner. It had been necessary to find someone with talent after the incident with the blood and...well, the rest was better left unremembered.

Chief Bradley towered over his oak desk. It was cluttered with pictures of his family and at least three coffee mugs, all proclaiming him *World's Best Grandpa*. Behind him was a screen built into the wall that showed all the active cases in his division – murders, robberies, and organized crime, all committed by supernaturals. The room smelled faintly of cigars.

"A vampire walked out in broad daylight and blew up," Bradley said, tossing the picture of the graphic crime scene down on a thick folder. "The morning after *robbing a bank* in Seattle."

"A bank? That's odd," I commented, grimacing as I looked at the picture. One of her legs had managed to land in a trash can, her heeled foot sticking up like a demented candlestick.

Vampires weren't vulnerable to much, but they could not tolerate sunlight. An old prosaic myth was that they burned in the sun. I wish that was all they did. Instead, they exploded. The pieces would smolder and burn into ash eventually, but it was a messy way to go.

"This is a PR disaster," Bradley continued, his voice growing in volume. "The Vampire Guild is up in arms, the Mayor of Seattle is stirring the prosaics up about the supposed supernatural threat, and I haven't even had my coffee yet."

He stood with his fists on his hips waiting for our reaction. The pink-haired woman was sitting in the chair next to me, but Bradley hadn't bothered introducing her.

I still wondered what her purpose was here. She couldn't be a detective with *that* hair. Besides, I'd never seen her before. If I had, I would already have her number. Maybe I could get it after this and arrange a different kind of meeting. One that involved drinks and less clothes.

I leaned forward and grabbed the file off the table. "No signs of aggression or blood psychosis, but the ME's initial ruling is still just suicide," I commented as I flipped through the file. "If she robbed a bank this was probably a less painful death. The Vampire Guild would have killed her slow for pulling a stunt like that."

"Perhaps, but there's always a reason when a supernatural dies," the pink-haired woman stated, turning to look at me. "Especially a vampire over two hundred years old. It's lazy to assume it's a suicide without investigating it at all."

A muscle in my jaw twitched as I clenched my teeth tightly together. "I've been accused of a lot of things, lady, but lazy is never one of them," I drawled, trying not to let on to the extent of my irritation. "Why is she even in here? This is a police matter, not fashion week." I gestured at her outfit, just in case Bradley had somehow missed it. She might be hot, but she was getting on my nerves. I had my issues, but I was a good detective.

"Ah, that brings me to the other reason I asked you in here," Bradley said, a smug look settling on his face.

I didn't like it. Any reason Bradley had to look smug always meant pain and annoyance for me. I narrowed my eyes at him threateningly, but that just made his smug smile grow.

"This is your new partner, Detective Lexi Swift," Bradley said, hooking his thumbs into his waistband.

"My what?" I demanded, slamming my hands down on his desk and rising to my feet.

"You heard me," Bradley said, full-on grinning now. "After last week's fiasco, I was forced to find a solution for you. You're the best detective we have, but you leave a trail of destruction and chaos behind you. Frankly, the department can't take it anymore."

"I do what I have to in order to get the job done—"

Bradley lifted his hand, cutting me off. "No more excuses, Blackwell. You're working with Swift. She was the best detective they had in Magical Artifacts, but more importantly, she had no complaints last year."

That explained never meeting her; those agents were often posted in places other than Moira. That whole division was made up of nerds who fancied themselves a cross between librarian and archeologist.

I turned my glare on her and she stared back impassively. I seriously regretted even considering buying her a drink at this point. Talk about dodging a bullet. "I work alone," I snapped. "And all those complaints were crap and you know it!"

"You blew up the front of the Met! You've been banned from New York City for a year!" Bradley yelled, his patience finally cracking. "And that was after you led a high-speed chase through three cities and Moira! There was over five million dollars in property damage! You're getting a damn partner, and if I get one more damn complaint about you, you're suspended! Without pay!" Bradley said, slamming his hands down on the desk and matching my glare.

"I paid for the damages," I said, grinding my teeth

together. "And you know I don't give a crap about the paycheck!"

"Suspended means no cases," Bradley said, jabbing a finger in my face.

I pressed my lips into a thin line, and Bradley leaned back, self-satisfied. He knew he had won. There was a reason I worked when I had more money than I could ever spend, even in my extended lifetime – interest is a beautiful thing. My parents had been murdered over one hundred and thirty years ago. I needed this job if I ever hoped to catch the people responsible. Political assassinations were convoluted and messy affairs, but supernaturals had long memories; and we could hold a grudge better than anyone. The contacts and the skills I had gained brought me one step closer to that goal every day.

Swift uncurled from her chair, her eyes sparking with anger. Literally. "I knew you had a reputation, Blackwell, but you're even worse than I expected," she said, those pretty lips dripping with disdain. She turned to Bradley and a mask of professionalism fell over her features. "I'm sure Detective Blackwell and I will have an effective partnership, even if I have to do all the work myself."

"Like hell, we will," I muttered, snatching the folder off the desk. "This conversation isn't over, Chief."

"You better not be in my office in the morning trying

to complain," Bradley threatened as I turned and shoved the door open.

A whiff of Swift's perfume tickled my nose as I brushed past her. The scent followed me as I strode through the department. The other detectives were used to my moods and my temper; they stayed out of my way and kept quiet.

Swift followed me out of Bradley's office and out of the station. In fact, she followed me all the way down to the Rune Ride rental office. Maybe if I ignored her long enough she would take the hint and go away.

"Hey, Billy," I said, nodding at the kid behind the rental desk.

Rune Ride was one small part of MR, Incorporated, the massive international company that owned and operated Moira. Lucky for me, MR, Inc. had worked out a deal with IMIB that let us travel for free, even off duty. That included rental vehicles. You picked up the keys in Moira for the car available in the region you were traveling to, then just found it in the garage. It streamlined the process and allowed them to keep minimal staff in the many cities the Rune Rail reached.

"Hey, Blackwell," Billy said, grinning and waving his tablet at me. "The usual?"

"Absolutely," I said with a nod.

Bobby grabbed the key he hid under the counter for me and handed it over. I slid my company card across the desk, but instead of taking it, he was staring slack-jawed over my shoulder. At Swift.

I snapped my fingers in front of his face and he startled out of it. "Dude, don't ogle the enemy," I chastised him.

"The enemy?" Bobby whispered, his eyes going wide.

"Yeah, she's an evil parasite I can't get rid of," I explained, shoving my card at him. "Let's hurry it up, kid."

Swift snorted behind me. The first reaction I'd gotten out of her. "What is the usual?" she asked, stepping up beside me and grabbing the key off the counter.

I snatched it out of her hands before she could get a good look. "Don't worry about it, I'll be driving," I said, slipping the key Bobby kept hidden for me in my pocket. I'm a particular guy. I like certain cars, my suits to be impeccable, and always getting my way. That's why I work alone.

Swift rolled her eyes. "I'm surprised you manage to get anything done with that attitude."

"I get plenty done," I said, striding off toward the platform that would take us to Seattle. The vampires favored that area because of its severe lack of sunlight.

Moira had forty levels, counting from the bottom up like a high-rise building. The Rune Rail system took up the lower eight, and was divided up by the region it serviced. North America was on level seven.

There's an old saying about Moira, *the higher you go, the more it costs*. The top few levels were filled with mansions for the rich, famous, and powerful. In between, Moira was filled with shopping and entertainment.

Swift kept up with me easily despite my quick pace and longer legs. "Do you have any contacts in Seattle?" Swift asked. "Because if not, I know some people we can speak with to get some more information on the local vampire activity."

"How about we figure out if this is a suicide first," I said drily. "And I know plenty of people in Seattle we can get information from, if we need to, and that's a big if."

Swift grabbed my arm and forced me to a stop. She was stronger than she looked, but most of our kind were. "Look, I didn't want to get stuck with you any more than you wanted to be stuck with me. But we're partners now and it's stupid to work against each other, when we can be more effective as a team."

I jerked my arm out of her grip. "You're going to get in my way," I said, looking directly into her creepy, glowing eyes. "In fact, you already have."

I'm sure she was competent, and even smart, but having a partner was a risk I wasn't willing to take. The assassins who had come for me this morning had been crappy; but if someone else had been there, I might not have been able to protect them. I hadn't been able to last time I had a partner.

She pursed her lips and looked at me thoughtfully. "How about a wager then, to prove who is the better detective."

"And how are we going to prove who is better?" I asked, raising my brow.

"If this turns out to be a suicide, you win, and I'll ask for a transfer," Swift said. "If it's murder, then you have to dye your hair pink until we solve the case."

There was no way in hell I would ever dye my hair pink; but there was also no way I was backing down from this wager, even if it was dumb and risky. "Fine, you have a deal, Swift."

She stuck out her hand with a glint in her eyes. I wrapped my fingers around hers, and the magic from our pact bound our hands together in golden threads that shone brightly before disappearing with a snap.

Magic was a finicky thing. When two supernaturals made an important agreement, it bound them to it. The consequences for going back on your word were unpredictable. I hadn't expected our magic to bind a silly wager like this.

A bad feeling settled in my gut. I didn't like the smug look in her eyes anymore than I liked seeing it on Bradley. Our train popped up next to the platform, a puff of air rushing past us.

“Ladies first,” I mocked, waving her ahead of me with a bow.

She snorted and brushed past me. “You’re going to look ridiculous with pink hair,” she said over her shoulder.

FOUR

The alarm beeped twice as I unlocked the matte-black Nissan GT-R I always drove. It had a V6, six hundred horsepower engine, and a six-speed transmission. The little beauty did 0 to 100 km/h in 3.4 seconds. But my runetech model did double that. It was a dream car. A technological marvel. And as far as I was concerned, it was mine.

"Seriously?" Swift asked. "That car is tiny."

"Don't insult my baby," I objected. "She's fast, and the trunk is runed to be five times bigger on the inside."

Swift still looked skeptical, but she climbed in the passenger seat without further complaint. The engine roared to life, a sound that never failed to put a grin on my face. This car was the only partner I needed.

"We should go see the coroner," Swift said. "It's on Third and Main."

"No," I said, throwing the car into first gear. "I always start at the crime scene."

"Do you always have to be in control?" Swift snapped in annoyance.

"I just like things done a certain way. My way." I winked at her, which prompted another eye roll. She was going to sprain something before the day was over.

"I see your reputation is well-deserved," she muttered.

I just grinned and screeched through the parking garage, enjoying a little speed while I could. It was evening rush hour in Seattle. It was also raining, but no surprise there.

"So, what kind of mage are you?" I asked, watching her in my periphery. The colorful pink eyes would normally indicate mage, but there were all sorts of weird cosmetic enhancements available these days.

"I read in your file that you're also a mage," Swift replied instead of answering the question.

"Who the hell gave you my file?" I demanded.

"Unlike you, I'm pleasant to people. That makes them more inclined to give answers when I ask questions," she said with a mocking smile.

I huffed and drifted through the next turn. Her shoulder bumped against the window and she glared at me.

The bank was in the middle of downtown. It was an old, three-story building. Next door was one of those high-class clothing stores that never had anyone in them but could sell one dress and stay open for three months.

A parking spot opened up right in front of the bank. I backed in; the day might have started off crappy, but my luck was improving.

We walked through the newly replaced glass doors of the bank. They had the air conditioning on full blast; if I hadn't been wearing a suit jacket, I would have been cold.

The bank wasn't exactly bustling with activity. A few customers were inside, but they were all being directed to a single teller far away from the damaged area.

Swift headed straight for the vault, but I trailed behind her, taking in the locations of the cameras. The place was covered in them. I'd bet there wasn't a single square inch that wasn't monitored twenty-four seven.

A man who was almost as wide as he was tall hurried across the floor. Swift slowed when she saw him, but almost walked past when he stopped in front of her. I picked up my pace and walked up behind them to listen in to their conversation.

The little metal nametag pinned to his suit read Howard E. Barnes, with Bank Manager in all caps underneath.

"Ms. Swift," he said, slightly breathless from his fast walk over here. "I attempted to call the number we had on file, but it seems to have been disconnected. I am so glad to see you here. I wanted to assure you, in person, that your accounts and personal lockbox were completely unaffected by the incident night before last." His cheeks were flushed with either embarrassment or nerves, possibly both.

"That's good to hear, sir. However, I'm actually here on business. I work for the IMIB now, and my partner, Detective Blackwell, and I are investigating the robbery," Swift said, gesturing at me and pasting a professional smile on her face.

"Oh, my apologies then," the manager said, turning even more red. He glanced at me and clasped his hands together. "Do you have any idea when we will be able to begin cleanup and repairs?"

Swift stiffened slightly; she didn't approve of his question for some reason. "Unfortunately, due to the involvement of a supernatural in the crime, we have to keep the crime scene available for a longer period. We can clear it for repairs in a couple of days, most likely."

"Ah, of course. I will leave you to your investigations. If you need anything at all, don't hesitate to ask. I will be in my office."

Swift nodded, and the squat man turned and puffed his way back across the floor.

"You must have a lot of money in here if the manager is running across the place to apologize to you," I teased.

Swift snorted. "My parents have money in this bank, I don't...well, anyhow, that's not important," she said, catching herself. It made me wonder if she was trying to hide something. "It's this way, they've photographed it but haven't started cleanup."

I came to an abrupt stop in front of the vault. The vampire had ripped huge chunks of concrete out of the wall, then ripped the safe door off its hinges. Now, vampires were strong, but most didn't have that kind of strength. She would have injured herself busting through that much concrete. The injuries would have healed quickly, especially if she fed, but it would still have hurt.

The other thing bothering me was that vampires just didn't rob banks. They were strong enough to, but they had to be both young and stupid to try. The Vampire Guild would have their head on a stake faster than they could blink when they caught them. It really was looking like a suicide.

Everybody, including vampires and shifters, were still afraid of the Mage's Guild coming down on them. They were heavy-handed with their punishments, in an end the line and salt the earth kind of way. They didn't like supernaturals doing things that drew negative attention; peace with prosaics had been hard won, but surprisingly, their power had only grown since working with prosaics instead of hiding in the shadows. Humanity was a profitable market.

"The bank was robbed after closing, no fatalities other than the vampire the following morning," Swift said, ducking under the yellow police tape. She stepped through the rubble, her eyes scanning the damage. I followed her and crouched down to examine a large chunk of concrete.

"All this damage makes it seem like she was angry about something," I commented, standing back up.

"You'd think," Swift said, shaking her head. "She walked through the front door at two a.m. The cameras didn't catch much because she was moving too fast. She got into the safe one minute later and left with an estimated two million in cash. She didn't take everything that was there, just cash, and what was easily accessible. The whole robbery lasted less than four minutes. Perhaps it was efficiency, not anger, that drove her."

"Did she try to disguise herself at all?" I asked, looking over my shoulder at the closest camera.

"Nope. The camera across the street got a clear look at her face as she left, too," Swift said, pursing her lips. "She's efficient, getting out well before the police would have time to respond to the alarm, but then she walks out and basically looks into the camera across the street. Nothing about this case makes sense; it's like she wanted to get caught. I looked up her history earlier, and she was not new at this. Martina Bianchi is almost two-hundred years old, she's been involved with the mob her entire life, and she has a reputation as a cutthroat loan shark."

"Bianchi, hmm..." I repeated, rolling the name around in my mind. It was vaguely familiar, but I didn't think I had ever dealt with her directly. I had grown up bouncing between London, Tokyo, and New York City due to my parents' work. Since joining the IMIB a little over twenty years ago, I had spent more time dealing with the yakuza in Japan than I had anything in the States. "Is she affiliated with a vampire clan, or any of the mafia families?"

"Looks like her clan *is* one of the mafia families. She took over as the head of the family after her father died, in mysterious circumstances, shortly after she was changed. She has turned a few of her associates, but, for the most part, it's just another Italian mafia family," Swift explained.

"Any sign of the cash?" I asked.

"No, and according to the preliminary interviews, she came home for about an hour that night, but she didn't have the money. She wasn't carrying anything at all. Security at her loft confirms that."

"It could have been some kind of last act of revenge before she killed herself," I mused. Swift was convinced this was a murder, but I wasn't going to let go of the suicide angle until I had proof it was something else, especially since the fate of my hair rested on it.

My phone rang, and at the same time a police car flew by the bank, sirens wailing.

"Blackwell," I said, answering the call.

"We've got a robbery in progress at a jewelry store awfully close to the first crime scene. It's a werewolf, completely out of control," Bradley's voice boomed through the tinny speakers of the phone. "Get your asses over there and arrest this thing before it gets away. The local PD isn't equipped to handle something like this."

"Got it, boss," I said, gesturing for Swift to follow me as I jogged toward the exit.

"And don't blow anything up," he warned.

"Whatever you say, boss." A grin spread across my face. It was so tempting to do it when he ordered me not to like that.

"Blackwell, I mean it--"

"Gotta go," I said, hanging up the phone before he could get started on a rant. I didn't have the patience, or time, for that nonsense, especially after he stuck me with an unwanted partner.

"What's going on?" Swift demanded as we ran out to the car.

"Just a little fun to break up the monotony." I jumped

and slid over the hood of the car, landing nimbly on the other side.

Swift rolled her eyes and yanked the passenger door open. “Show off.”

“Don’t act like you’re not impressed.”

FIVE

I peeled out of the parking spot in front of the bank, leaving black streaks on the pavement. A patrol car skidded around a turn in front of me. I sped up until I was practically bumper to bumper with them and followed them toward the crime scene.

"Do you think this is related?" Swift asked.

"Why would it be?" I turned the wheel sharply; the car hugged the turn as if I were going twenty instead of fifty.

"Supernaturals robbing places are almost unheard of; now there's a second in the same city a day later? That's not a coincidence," Swift argued.

I gritted my teeth, but she was right. I didn't believe in coincidences, but I wasn't about to admit that to her. I should never have made that bet. It's something I would never have done if I'd stopped to think, but Bradley had dumped her on me and it had pissed me off. I didn't make my best decisions when I was mad. That was another reason I liked working alone; I was more focused.

The patrol car stopped abruptly. I swerved around it and parked past it, one wheel up on the curb. Swift leapt out of the car as a roar filled the air. The windows rattled with the force of it.

"They weren't kidding about out of control," I muttered as I locked the car and ran to catch up with Swift. A patrol officer holding a radio up to his ear was pointing at the building, his eyes wide.

"How bad is it?" I asked as I joined them.

"The place is trashed," the patrol officer said. "A SWAT team is on the way, but he's already killed at least two people and –"

"Look out!" Swift yelled, shoving me to the side. My ribs almost gave way from the force of her push. That was going to leave a bruise. She was *way* stronger than she looked.

A loud crash and the sound of broken glass drew my attention behind us. I looked back in horror. A huge, one hundred and thirty kilo man lay on the crushed remains of my precious, perfect car. Dead.

Swift sprinted into the building.

"Don't let SWAT in when they get here; they'll just get in our way," I warned the patrol officer before running in after her. I struggled to catch up to Swift; she was fast. Maybe it was a family trait. The screams grew louder and more panicked as I got closer.

SWAT was usually happy to let us handle supernatural issues. prosaic police took care of the humans, and we took care of anything related to magic. When cases crossed both lines...well...that did get messy sometimes.

Today was definitely going to get messy. For the body to crush the car like that, he had to have been thrown with the same amount of force as a fall from a ten-story building, even though it was only a two-story building. I was going to rip this werewolf apart for crushing my car like that.

Red emergency lights flashed throughout the store, glinting off the glass that littered the carpet. A man in a suit, an employee most likely, lay dead in a pool of blood. He was missing some important bits – like his right arm and throat. The arm was lying on the other side of the room.

The thick glass cases that protected the jewelry were all broken. Jewelry was strewn all over the floor in a trail leading toward the stairway to the second floor. Shiny breadcrumbs for us to follow, if the screaming and roaring weren't enough.

Swift held her hand out to the side and the sharp smell of magic, reminiscent of ozone, filled the air. With a bright pink pulse of light, a mace as big as she was materialized in her hand. The glinting metal hammer was covered in runes. I recognized a few: indestructibility, defense against magic, and one that made it weigh heavier, which was...unexpected. She dropped the end to the ground, and I felt the thump from a meter away.

"Of course, you're a berserker," I said, shaking my head. Swift might seem prim and proper right now, but berserker mages were crazy. And the crazy always showed eventually, normally at the worst possible moment.

A body flew into the hallway, denting the sheetrock. The man fell to the ground in an unconscious lump.

"I hate shifters," I said, taking off at a run toward the sounds of mayhem coming from the second story.

A werewolf, fully shifted in the middle of the day, roared its displeasure. The lanky, furry beast had one clawed hand wrapped around a screaming woman's leg, and the other around a chunk broken off a chair.

"IMIB! Drop the woman and the weapon!" I shouted, lifting one hand in preparation to cast, while the other rested on the hilt of my sword. There was no way this guy was going to listen, but I liked to give people a sporting chance to surrender peacefully.

A blur of pink and metal surged past me as Swift charged in, swinging the mace with one hand. The werewolf leapt out of the way and the mace hit the floor. The momentum of her swing caused the mace to slide across the floor, smashing through the tile as it went. I guess Swift was more attack first, demand surrender…never.

The werewolf flung the woman at me. I caught her just in time to avoid an elbow to the face but stumbled backward with the force of the throw.

"Get out of here," I shouted at her as I turned and dropped her on her feet, emphasizing my instruction with a hard shove toward the door. She ran off like her hair was on fire.

"I'll skin you and wear you as a fur coat!" Swift shouted as she swung the giant hammer straight at the werewolf. It caught her mace with one hand. The building shook with the shock of the impact. The werewolf smacked Swift with his other hand, sending her flying across the room.

I drew my katana as I ran toward him.

"Catch this, asshole!" I shouted, swinging the black blade at his hairy arm.

The werewolf roared and did, in fact, try to catch it. The blade sliced through his hand like butter, lopping off all four fingers and his thumb. The clawed digits fells to the floor, twitching. He stumbled backward with a high-pitched yelp as blood sprayed from his hand.

Swift's mace connected with his head and he went down. His skull was crushed between the tile and the heavy chunk of metal with a loud crunch. I cringed at the noise and took a step back.

Swift grinned at me, a wild look in her eyes. She jerked the mace free and gripped it with two hands. Blood dripped from the hem of her trench coat.

"Are you going to admit it wasn't a suicide now?" Swift taunted.

"Fine, there's something weird going on, but—" Magic tingled over my scalp and my retort died on my lips. I rushed over to a mirror dangling from the wall and ripped it free. My hair was pink.

I turned my glare on Swift. Tears of laughter streamed down her face.

SIX

The coroner's office smelled like Pop-Tarts and disinfectant. The combination had ruined Pop-Tarts for me years ago. Every time I looked at one, all I could think about were corpses.

Viktor strolled out from his tiny office, pulling on his white lab coat as he walked. He had an imposing presence, something about the combination of chiseled jaw and a hundred ninety-five centimeter frame put a guy on edge. I was pretty sure Viktor had wrestled a bear in his time, and won.

"Blackwell," Viktor said, his Russian accent drawing out my name. He pulled on a pair of blue latex gloves and glanced at Swift, who stood at my shoulder. "Why is your hair pink?"

I crossed my arms and ignored the snicker from

Swift. "I lost a bet," I ground out. "Do you have the remains of the vampire that took a daywalk?"

Viktor nodded. "I expected to see you much sooner on an odd case like this one."

"We got held up due to an unfortunate incident with a werewolf when we went to the crime scene. Surprisingly, it wasn't my fault this time," I explained with a grin.

Viktor snorted. "Yes, I heard. I have that corpse as well. I'm sure whatever happened would have been resolved with less property damage if you had not been there." He walked over to a metal table and pulled the white sheet back, revealing a pile of burnt chunks that used to be a vampire. She hadn't been reduced completely to ash, but the pieces that were left were… crumbly...and gooey. Lucky for us, her head had blown off instead of into pieces.

"Not much left to examine," Swift said, grimacing and turning her head away slightly, like that could lessen the awful scent of burnt flesh.

I'd seen that pained look on new agents' faces before; she hadn't been around many dead bodies, especially not any this gruesome.

"Who is this?" Viktor asked, narrowing his eyes at Swift. From his tone, I could tell she had already managed to insult him. She had no idea how little Viktor required to get information from a corpse.

"Detective Lexi Swift," I said, leaning over to look at the body. "Chief Bradley gave me a new partner."

"I transferred from Magical Artifacts," Swift said, extending her hand toward Viktor. "I'm supposed to keep Blackwell out of trouble."

Viktor stared at her impassively. "If you could move back, I will begin the examination."

I took a step back immediately, and, after another awkward moment, Swift gave up on the handshake and joined me. At least one of my friends hadn't decided they liked Swift better than me. Billy was a traitor.

"First dead body, Swift?" I whispered.

She shot a glare at me and pressed her hand to her nose and mouth. "I didn't exactly hang out at the morgue before. I've seen plenty of mummies though."

I raised my brow. "The recently dead are little different."

"Definitely smellier," she muttered before turning her attention back to Viktor.

Viktor arranged what was left of the blackened arms as though he were folding them across the vampire's chest, which was just a pile of red and black Jello at this point. Holding his hands out over the remains, he began to chant. His eyes went black, and darkness creeped through the veins on his face. He looked scary as hell when he did this.

The vampire's eyelids twitched. It was a subtle movement, small enough that you could almost write it off as your imagination. The arms convulsed, flopping on the table like a fish. Once. Twice. Then they were still.

Swift tensed beside me, her fingers twitching as if she wanted to summon her mace. I grabbed her arm and shook my head firmly. If she pulled something like that while Viktor was working his magic, there'd be hell to pay. The piney scent of frankincense filled the room, and the vampire's eyes snapped open.

The head wobbled as the grey-tinged eyes rolled around in the blackened skull. I suppressed a shudder; that was disgusting.

Swift made a weird noise in the back of her throat.

"Don't you dare throw up," I hissed at her. If she barfed, I might lose my cool.

"Ask your questions," Viktor said, his voice deeper than normal. A wisp of black smoke leaked from his lips.

"Martina," I said, drawing the vampire's attention. The creepy eyes snapped toward me, causing the head to tip over onto its side.

Swift swallowed audibly beside me. Chatting with the dead was always unnerving, but I pretended it didn't bother me.

"Why did you rob the bank?" I asked.

The vampire's jaw opened, leaving a wet streak on the steel table. The voice that replied wasn't hers – she had no lungs or vocal cords anymore. Instead, it was Viktor who spoke, his voice raspy and weirdly feminine.

"I don't...remember," the vampire replied through Viktor. Little bits of ash fell from her chin as it opened and shut in a sick imitation of speech. The sun had really done a number on her; she only had part of one lip left.

"You don't remember why, or you don't remember robbing it?" I prompted. Zombies were always a little short on the attention span. It was hard to keep them focused on the questions, and if you lost their attention too early on, the whole interrogation became a waste of time.

"Where am I?" she asked, avoiding the question. Viktor's nose twitched and her hand abruptly curled into a fist, causing the nails to screech against the metal. The noise made my ears ache and my skin crawl. I *hated* that sound.

As gross as it was, I was glad she was in pieces and couldn't walk around, not that Viktor would let that happen. Zombies were not allowed to get off the table, not even during an interrogation.

"You're dead and in the coroner's office. What is the last thing you remember?" I asked.

"Dead?" the girl asked. "That's odd. I'm still hungry."

I glanced at Viktor. He shrugged, but a frown tugged

at his lips. "You can have a nice cup of blood if you answer my questions," I said.

"I'd rather have something else..." the woman said, her charred face seeming to brighten with excitement. She blinked rapidly, and the head wobbled as her teeth clicked together as if she were chewing.

The sight of a burnt, severed head chewing like that was going to haunt my nightmares forever. "Sure, whatever you want," I lied to get her to stop making that awful noise. "Now, tell me what's the last thing you remember?"

"I was walking home around midnight, and I heard something odd," the vampire said. Viktor's nose twitched again. "Then everything went sideways. Now I'm here. Can I have something to eat now? Human food?"

"Just one more question," Swift interjected. "What did you smell right before you died?"

Martina's face contorted into a grimace, and another chunk of her eyebrow plopped onto the table. "Something stinky."

Swift pinched her brows together and looked at me. "That's odd."

When she didn't finish her thought, I raised my brow. "Well?"

Swift shook herself out of her thoughts. "If it's not

some kind of psychotic break, it seems like a possession. I have no idea what could, or would, even want to possess a vampire though. Demons haven't been an issue for years.

"I'm so hungry," the vampire whined.

"We're done, Viktor," I said, wanting to avoid any more begging from the dead chick.

Viktor nodded and closed his hands. The vampire went still, freezing with the eyes open, but she was dead for good.

"Can we interrogate the werewolf," Swift flipped open her notebook to check his name, "Antonio Ricci, as well?"

"No," Viktor said, offended for a second time. "You crushed its head. I cannot reanimate a corpse without an intact brain."

Swift looked properly chagrined. "I'll keep that in mind when I'm detaining suspects in the future," she said.

"See that you do." Viktor pulled the sheet back over the vampire's remains then stripped off his gloves, tossing them in the trash.

"I'm sure we'll see you again soon, Viktor. Thanks for the help," I said, clapping him on the shoulder as I walked past.

"Anytime, Blackwell," Viktor said, narrowing his eyes at Swift as she followed me out of the morgue.

"I'm impressed you kept your lunch," I commented as we headed back to our area of the IMIB offices.

"If I can handle looking at that all day," she said, gesturing at my head, "then I can deal with a crispy, reanimated vampire."

I glared at her but decided the silent treatment was the safest option. My office was a quick elevator ride and short walk away.

We walked into the department, and I stopped in my tracks as a horrifying sight met my eyes. My desk was being carried out of my office, and two smaller desks sat outside, ready to be moved in.

"What the hell are you doing?" I demanded, striding toward the movers.

The mover froze. "Chief Bradley instructed us to tell you he was ordering you to clean your old desk out," he said. "There was no room for a second desk in there otherwise."

I ground my teeth together. They didn't have a choice. "This is all your fault," I said, turning my glare on Swift.

She grinned and strode toward the office, completely unconcerned. I followed, and cleaned my desk out while the whole department watched. My irritation grew with every piece of paper I had to move.

"We need to go through Martina Bianchi's house," Swift said, tapping her foot impatiently.

"It's probably 10:00 p.m. in Seattle right now. Unlike Moira, the city does shut down at night," I said, slamming the last drawer shut. "I'm calling it a day."

Swift huffed in irritation but didn't bother arguing. "Fine, I'll see you bright and early in the morning, partner."

SEVEN

The faces of the victims, Martina Bianchi, vampire mafia matriarch, and Antonio Ricci, her ruthless – and now pancake-faced – werewolf enforcer, hovered at the top of the large screen that was built into the walls of the conference room.

The System, as we called it, was relatively new technology that had rolled out a few years back. In the past, we had whiteboards where we taped up the pictures of victims and suspects and wrote out notes; now I could access all of that electronically. Everything was connected, with user permissions dictating who could see what. They claimed it was un-hackable, which to me sounded more like they had thrown down a challenge; but for four years they'd been right.

I flicked my finger lazily across my tablet, and the list of their crimes popped up below their faces. The lists were...not short. "Who are her biggest rivals?" I asked. "We should start there. They'd have the most to gain from her death."

"Not her own family? Her son is named as her successor; but if he wanted to take over the business, he would have to wait a long time if dear old mom was near-immortal," Swift said, swiveling in her chair to face me. She typed something on her tablet, which was connected to the screen, and the son's picture and criminal history appeared to the left of Martina's. There wasn't much there surprisingly.

"We can check on that, too, but her family was stable. Loyal. I think it's more likely it was an outsider," I said with a shrug. Whether because she was a vampire, or a good leader, she had kept her family together without incident for over two hundred years. That was impressive.

"Everyone thinks their family is loyal until they get stabbed in the back. Look," she pointed at the screen with her tablet, "she turned her son almost fifty years ago, but she's kept him on the fringes of the business. That has to have pissed him off."

I walked over to the electronic board and tapped on his name, which then showed his recent affiliations. Charity. Marketing. Funding start-ups. I snorted, "Maybe it would piss you off, but it looks more like he chose not to get involved in the mafia stuff. For a vampire, he's basically a saint." I turned back to face her and slipped my hands into the pockets of my slacks. "Sounds like you're projecting."

Swift's face hardened and her pink eyes glinted with magic. If looks could kill, I'd be a pile of ash. "I was right about the suicide; maybe you could take my observations seriously instead of being dismissive," Swift said, her fingers digging into the edge of her tablet.

"It's not dismissive to prove you're wrong," I said, flopping down in my chair. The muscle in Swift's jaw twitched as she ground her teeth together.

"I'll pull up a file on everyone who's affiliated with organized crime in Seattle, but we are going to talk to her son," she insisted.

"Fine, but it's a waste of time," I shrugged. That wasn't actually true. It was necessary, even if it was just to rule him out as a suspect. I wasn't ever that sloppy, but the urge to disagree with Swift was just too strong sometimes. Eventually, she'd give up on this partnership and ask for a transfer, then things could get back to normal.

She muttered something, probably insulting, under her breath before jabbing at her tablet again. The System began compiling a list of people known to be involved in organized crime in the region. "As for the rival angle, it could be someone new trying to make a name for themselves, or take over her territory. What we really need is to be able to talk to someone involved with the mafia around here. You know anyone that would help us out, or do I need to take care of that too?" Swift asked.

"Maybe," I replied, tapping my fingers against the mahogany table top as I tried to mentally talk myself out of the first idea that had come to mind. I knew someone all right, but talking to him was not advisable.

"Either you do, or you don't," Swift said.

"I'll let you know if he's available for questions tomorrow." I stood and straightened my suit jacket. "Let's go to their houses and take a look around. We can't make any more progress sitting around in here."

"I'll make an appointment with Alberto Bianchi if I can, even if I have to go alone." Swift slapped the cover of her tablet shut so hard I had to wonder if she'd cracked it. "I guess we have to walk from the Rune Rail Station to their houses since your dinky little car got crushed."

I smirked at her. "What's the problem? Are your boots not made for walking?"

EIGHT

Martina Bianchi lived in a condo in downtown Seattle. The place had been taped off as a crime scene while the search warrant was served. With two million in cash missing, there was no way the IMIB would let the family back in this place before the money was found.

I nodded at the patrol officer who was stationed at the door, then ducked under the yellow tape and took in the room. Clean, modern, and well lit for a place with no windows. A screen that took up the entire back wall showed the view the condo should have had. The Space Needle glinted in the distance, towering over the surrounding buildings.

I pulled on the blue latex gloves we were required to wear at crime scenes as I walked toward the kitchen. It had been converted to a game room; the only remaining amenity for any human visitors was a mini-fridge and a microwave. A massive sectional with enough room for a dozen people was arranged around the screen in the living area.

Sergeant Lopez walked out of the bedroom, casting a confused glance at Swift but stopping in her tracks when she saw me. She crossed her arms and cocked her head. "Detective Blackwell, interesting look," she said in greeting. Lopez was a short woman with dark-brown hair and eyes the same color. Her round face made her look approachable, soft even, but I had quickly learned that was not the case.

I ran my hands through the pink strands on my head. "I lost a bet."

"You? Lost a bet?" Lopez said, grinning like the cat that got the cream. "Who managed to get one over on you?"

"I did," Swift said walking up to her. "Detective Lexi Swift," she said extending her hand to Lopez. "I'm Blackwell's new partner."

"Sergeant Camila Lopez," she said, shaking her hand and looking at her appraisingly. Lopez had joined the IMIB only two years ago, but she had been promoted up fast. She was some kind of shifter, though I had no idea what type, and it was rude to ask. She should have been a detective already with intelligence, but the rules dictated five years with the IMIB before you could be promoted up to that rank. Lucky for me, that meant she assisted me on cases. She was as close to a partner as I had had for the past two years, ever since my previous partner, Detective Anthony Granger, was killed.

"This doesn't look like the kind of place a vampire on the verge of blood psychosis would live," Swift commented as she opened the door to one of the bedrooms.

"Nope," Lopez agreed, looking around the place. "There's no sign of the money she stole either. Security logs her coming back that night after she robbed that bank, but she didn't bring it with her. We've been over this place with a fine-tooth comb. I put in a request to punch a few holes in the walls to check in there, but it was denied."

I snorted. That was Lopez for you. "I'm surprised you didn't do it anyway."

"Not all of us can get away with destroying stuff like you can, Detective," she said, glancing at my hair again. "Glad to see you've got someone to keep you in line now."

Swift grinned. "He looks awful in pink, doesn't he?" she said, winking at Lopez, who busted out laughing.

I groaned and turned away from the two women. Just what I needed, Swift recruiting all my coworkers to give me hell. I walked into the bathroom and dug through the cabinets and drawers, but there was no sign of illicit drugs, or even legal ones. The whole place was tidy and cozy, nothing like what I had expected.

Vampires that went feral always had warning signs. They would nest, tearing up blankets and pillows to build a safe place for their mates. Then, they would become aggressive and territorial, especially toward other vampires. Finally, they would start killing people. The cause was usually starvation, or severe over-feeding, but that sort of thing hardly ever happened anymore. Whatever Bianchi's issue had been, blood psychosis was definitely not it.

"It's like she snapped out of nowhere," Swift said, appearing at the bathroom door.

"There had to have been a reason," I said, rubbing my hand along my jaw. "She didn't remember anything, so someone else had to have made her rob that bank."

Swift stared at the floor, her eyes distant.

"What are you thinking?" I prompted.

"I'm not sure yet. Let's go check out the werewolf's place. I'm curious if we'll see the same thing there." Swift turned and headed back into the main area of the condo.

I lingered in the bathroom. The only thing out of place was a comb on the edge of the sink. I picked it up, and a long black hair clung to the teeth.

"Lopez, can you bag this and get it tested?" I asked, striding out of the bathroom. "Bianchi had brown hair, not black. Could be a friend, or a date, but I'd like to know for sure. Give me a call when you get the results."

"Will do, boss man," she said, carefully taking the edge of the comb with her gloved hand.

While Martina Bianchi had been old money, her enforcer was not. She paid him well, but his choice in condo and decor was...different. It was the kind of place you called a bachelor pad, if you were being polite; and, if you were being honest, the house of a man that could only offer a woman money.

The center of the room was dominated by a huge fountain. In the middle of that was a...pillar...spurting water a third of a meter into the air.

"Somebody is overcompensating," Swift said as she looked around the room. The living area had a massive u-shaped sectional around the biggest television I'd ever seen.

Everything in the house was bigger, or more expensive, than it needed to be. He even had two refrigerators. Granted, werewolves ate a whole lot more than humans or mages, but it was still overkill.

I opened the closest refrigerator. It was mostly beer and meat fresh from the butcher, except for a package with something familiar – onigiri. Based on the other things Ricci seemed to like, that was an odd choice.

"Hungry, Blackwell?" A deep voice rumbled behind me.

I turned to see Sergeant Danner, an old mage who looked more like a homeless person than an IMIB agent. He squinted at my hair but didn't comment on it. Danner had a motto: if it ain't my problem, it ain't my problem. Redundant, but it meant he did his job and went home and never had any problems with anyone.

"No, but I'm wondering if our victim had company right before he died," I said, stepping back and pointing at the Japanese food.

Danner pursed his lips and shrugged. "We dusted this whole place, no recent prints other than Ricci's."

Swift appeared behind us. "What did you find?"

"Not much," I said, jabbing my thumb at the onigiri. "Any signs of a struggle?"

"None," Swift said, shaking her head. "The place isn't exactly spotless, but there's nothing like that."

"Maybe he just snapped," Danner mused, gnawing on a toothpick that I swore hadn't been in his mouth two seconds ago. I hadn't seen him move, though. I was starting to suspect he just kept them in his cheeks like some kind of grizzled chipmunk.

"I'd believe that, if it weren't for the vampire," I said, rubbing the back of my hair in irritation. If I had waited just a few more minutes to get more details on the case and hadn't been distracted by having a new partner dumped in my lap, I wouldn't have taken that stupid bet.

"Then it has to be possession," Swift said. "It's the only thing left that makes any sort of sense, especially with the werewolf doing the same thing. A demon might go on a random killing spree like this, but I haven't ever heard of one jumping from person to person, much less possessing supernaturals."

I pinched the bridge of my nose. "All right, say I agree with that. We'll have to narrow down what might be possessing him and if a rival is controlling them somehow."

"I have a contact that can help with this," Swift said, looking like she wanted to say *I told you so*.

"Fine, but if he leaks any of this, it's on your head."

Swift shrugged. "Sounds good to me."

NINE

I hung up the phone from my aggravating conversation with Rune Ride. Apparently, they weren't keen on rushing a replacement car to me after the one I had was demolished. I hated the public transportation system in Seattle, so the buses were out. I also hated other people driving, so a cab was out of the question as well.

"We're going to have to walk back," I announced, shoving my phone back in my pocket.

"It's three kilometers back to the Rune Rail," Swift protested.

"Guess you should have worn more comfortable shoes," I said with a smirk, gesturing at Swift's heeled boots.

She rolled her eyes. "Or we could take the bus."

"The buses are slow here. We'll miss the Rune Rail," I

said, turning and starting down the street. We wouldn't, but I was not going to suffer through a bus ride at this time of day.

Swift jogged to catch up and fell in step beside me. "I'm going to get in touch with the contact I mentioned. We should be able to meet with him day after tomorrow. He's an expert in possessions; he should be able to tell us what is doing this," Swift said.

"Who is this guy, anyhow?" I asked as we crossed the street. "We can't give details of the case to every random person you just happen to know."

"Obviously, Blackwell," Swift said, exasperated. "This is someone I worked closely with for years when I was in Magical Artifacts. He's an old family friend and he's trustworthy, not to mention an expert in his field."

The scent of coffee drifted out of the door that opened ahead of us. One of the few things I liked about Seattle was the coffee shops on every corner. I had a caffeine addiction that I had no intention of ever quitting.

I ducked into the store and Swift followed me. "Coffee break already?" she asked, looking around the mostly empty building. Ten a.m. on a Tuesday wasn't exactly their busiest time, lucky for me.

"It's never too early for a coffee break," I said, stepping up to the counter.

"What can I get you?" the barista asked. Her fingers

hovered over the screen as she waited for my order with a bored expression.

"Matcha, hot, but at fifty-seven degrees celsius, with almond milk, an extra scoop of matcha, and one pump of classic syrup," I rattled off, waiting for her brain to catch up.

She tapped at the screen then squinted up at me. "Sorry, could you repeat that?" she asked.

I gritted my teeth and repeated the entire order, slower this time. I slid my card across the counter, hoping she had gotten most of it correct at least.

"I should have known you were the type to have an overly complicated drink order," Swift said, raising an eyebrow and looking at my perfectly tailored suit.

"I know what I like. Why should I have it any other way?" I asked.

She snorted. "I didn't really take you for the type to like green tea either. That stuff makes me gag."

"I spent a lot of time in Tokyo, and I fell in love with it, along with real sushi and wagyu beef," I said, as I took back my card from the barista. "Japan has great food."

"You'll fit right in on Harajuku now," Swift said with a smirk.

I resisted the urge to cover my hair. Even with a hat, I wouldn't be able to hide the horrendous pink. I hated magic sometimes. "You already knew it wasn't suicide when you conned me into that bet," I said, grabbing my hot matcha from the counter. I could tell just from holding the cup that it was way over one thirty-five.

"I don't make bets I'm not sure I'm going to win," Swift said, looking smug.

I stalked out of the cafe and tried to walk fast enough to leave Swift behind. Unfortunately, that was a lost cause. I blew on the tea; it was going to take forever to cool off. Most mages could use magic to cool it, but I always ended up overdoing it, and then I was stuck with a block of matcha-flavored ice.

"Is there any other information you're keeping to yourself?" I asked. "I'd like to get this case solved as quickly as possible."

"I bet you would…" Swift let her retort trail off as her eyes focused on someone in the distance.

"What?" I asked, immediately scanning the area for danger.

"I think we should run," Swift said, her voice tense.

"Why—"

A blast of arcane energy smacked me across the face. My cup of steaming hot matcha splattered all over my shirt and suit, burning the skin underneath. Before I had a chance to curse whoever had cast the spell, I was hit with a burst of air that knocked me flat on my back.

TEN

The world tilted as Swift leapt over my prone form. Her mace collided with an arcane bolt, and the impact exploded outward in a blaze of purple and pink light. My ears popped and all I could hear was ringing.

"I'll rip the flesh from your bones you worthless peons!" Swift shouted down the street. Her voice sounded muffled after the blast my eardrums had suffered. She twirled her mace over her head, cackling like a banshee.

And there was the crazy. I crumpled my empty cup and tossed it to the side. My ears were still ringing, but other than a sore backside, I was uninjured. I pushed up to a crouch and slapped my hand against the ground.

A force field rippled out with me at the epicenter. Swift leapt forward and bounced off the shield. It kept magic and people out, but kept us trapped in here as well, as long as it was active. It could be broken, but it would take a lot of power and at least a few minutes. I needed a second to figure out who was attacking us, and why. Assassins had already come after me this morning; it wasn't normal to be attacked twice in one day. I hadn't pissed anyone off *that* bad recently.

A mage approached, blue flames crawling up her arm as she eyed the shield around us. A long black trench coat billowed around her legs. Her head was shaved and inked with runic designs.

"Let me out of here," Swift snapped, whirling on me.

"What the hell do you want?" I demanded, stepping between Swift and the other mage.

"Move away from the girl and you may live," the bald chick threatened.

"You're after Swift?" I asked, incredulous, and a little insulted. My name was pretty well known among the undesirable types. Why would they be after Swift and not me?

"Hiring an inept bodyguard was a bad choice, Lexi," the mage said. The flames around her arm grew until they were too bright to look at directly. "You will both die, today!"

Swift shoved me to the side. "Let me out of here, Blackwell. This isn't your fight."

"I'm not going to just lower the shield," I snapped.

The mage lifted her hand and blue fire raced toward us. The initial impact sent splinters cracking across the force field. I stepped back, my eyes going wide. I had never seen a shield damaged from one blow before.

The second blast shattered it. The kickback from my magic imploding knocked me flat for a second time. Swift shouted something unintelligible as she rushed forward. Pink flames whipped out from her mace, smashing into the other mage.

They clashed, sparks flying between them. Swift caught a kick to the stomach and flew backwards. She used her mace to slowly drag herself to a stop and ran forward again.

I drew my sword and rushed in from the other side. A second mage I hadn't noticed before jumped into my path. I lifted my sword just in time, cutting through the arcane energies they cast. I swung quickly, going on the offensive before they could follow up to their original attack.

The guy looked like a rocker reject with the same trench coat and tattooed, bald head as his partner. He was fast; I'd give him that, but he wasn't as powerful as the chick.

I snapped my fingers and flames circled my hands. It was a defensive spell that packed a punch. Most mages didn't know what the flames did either. It was old school, something my master had taught me when I first started training under him.

The mage surged forward, sending a blast of arcane magic straight toward my face. Fire flared around my fist, acting as a guard, and I smacked the arcane magic out of the way with one hand before slashing at his midsection. He blocked the strike with a crackling line of pure arcane energy. The flames that circled my wrists billowed out in a bright gust.

The mage faltered and I twisted my wrists, ready to skewer him, when a blast of blue fire caught my attention. I lifted one arm to fend off the attack, but the blast hit me like a battering ram.

I groaned and lifted my cheek off the grimy concrete as I regained consciousness. Swift grabbed me by the shoulder and lifted me back onto my feet one-handed. She still had her mace in the other and was looking down the street suspiciously. The two mages that had attacked us lay still on the ground, but I couldn't tell if they were dead or not.

"We need to go," Swift said, her tone urgent.

"Who are those people?" I asked, wiping away blood that dripped from my nose.

"Don't worry about it," Swift said.

I jerked my shoulder out of her grip. "Don't worry about it? Seriously?" I exclaimed. "We were just attacked in broad daylight by two well-above-average mages. That is not a don't-worry-about-it situation, Swift."

"Look, I won't tell everyone you got knocked on your ass if you don't tell everyone we were attacked," Swift said, glaring at me.

"This is not going to go unnoticed," I said, waving my hand at the crowd watching from a safe distance.

"No one knows it was us, and if we get out of here now, no one will. Do we have a deal or not?" Swift asked.

"Fine," I ground out. She was coming out on top in way too many of these deals. "But I'm not taking the blame for this, and you're explaining this to me later."

"Fine," Swift snapped. "Let's go."

ELEVEN

Swift was waiting for me outside the men's locker room when I emerged in a fresh suit. Getting the coffee stain out earlier hadn't been a big deal, but matcha, skid marks from the asphalt, and the giant tear on the sleeve of the jacket were beyond my skills. I'd have to take the suit to my tailor.

"I told you I was calling it a day," I said, stopping in front of her.

"I was waiting to escort you home," Swift said, pushing off the wall. "You might be a target now, and I'd feel better if I knew you got home safely."

I laughed until I realized she was being completely serious. "You are not walking me home," I said shaking my head. "But you can explain who hates you so much that they would want to kill not only you, but anyone who happens to be associated with you."

"I have to get permission from Chief Bradley to brief you on those details," Swift said, jutting out her chin stubbornly.

"So you're not going to hold up your part of the deal?" I asked, irritation turning into justified anger. If Bradley knew she was being targeted for assassination, he should have told me. *She* should have told me.

Swift looked away. "I said I would explain, I never said when."

I shook my head and scoffed at her weak attempt at deflection. "You knew what I meant." When Swift remained silent, I decided that I had put up with enough ridiculous crap for one day, turned on my heel, and walked away. If she was going to keep secrets that put my life, and my best suits, at risk, then I would have to get the information on my own. Tomorrow, though. After a good night's sleep.

My apartment in Kichijoji was a thirty-five minute train ride from the Tokyo Rune Rail station. I held onto the handrail overhead and tried to ignore the press of bodies all around me. Other than the occasional handsy pervert that I had to smack for trying to grope a woman, everyone was polite and quiet despite being crammed together. The efficiency of the Tokyo train system was why I hated public transportation in every other city. Nothing else compared, and I had no patience for it.

The train came to a gentle stop and I squeezed out with the rush of other passengers. I hurried up the escalator and out onto the bustling street. It was the middle of the day in Kichijoji, even though it was well past dinner back in Seattle. My sleep schedule was a mess, to say the least. Since I did most of my work in North America, I had hung black-out curtains in my windows ages ago so that the sun didn't bother me while I slept.

The tension in my shoulders relaxed as I walked down the familiar streets. No one knew where I lived except the HR department. Every time I made it here, some of the constant wariness lifted. Not all of it, of course. I wasn't stupid. No one was ever completely safe.

I shoved my hand in my pocket to see how much yen I had on me. My favorite izakaya was on my way home, and I definitely didn't feel like cooking; but they only took cash.

I stopped mid-step as an alarmingly strong sense of magic tickled the edges of my senses. Most people suppressed their magical signature. It was considered rude to go around broadcasting your level of power, kind of like walking around with both middle fingers in the air.

The street ahead was mostly empty. I turned slowly,

putting my back to the wall so no one could creep up behind me. A woman, not Japanese but possibly American, with long black hair and thick bangs, walked slowly toward me. The power I was feeling came from her; of that I was certain.

"Logan Blackwell," she said, looking me up and down before dismissing me as uninteresting. "I've come as a courtesy, to warn you to stay out of our way."

"You're going to have to be more specific," I said, lifting an eyebrow. "I'm in a lot of people's way."

The woman did not look amused. "I am going to kill Lexi Swift, and if you try to stop me, I'll have no problem killing you as well."

What was with that chick? Everyone and their uncle seemed to want her dead. I couldn't deny that I was a little insulted that no one had ever put out this amount of effort to kill me. I had worked really hard to be a pain in the butt to every major criminal organization I came across. Yet, no one had sent mages of *this* caliber to kill me.

"Lady, I have no idea who you are, or why you want my partner dead; and I hate to disappoint new friends, but you're not killing Swift," I said, resting one hand on my katana. I didn't exactly like Swift, but she was still my partner and I couldn't have her wind up dead on my watch.

My fingers itched to blast this chick, but for once I

wasn't sure it was a fight I'd win. Well, I could definitely kill her, but I didn't count a fight as a win unless I got to walk away alive.

"So be it. I have fulfilled my obligation to warn you. The consequences of ignoring this warning will be on your head," the woman said, turning to walk away.

"Hey," I said, shouting after her. "Who are you?"

She glanced back over her shoulder and snorted. "There's no point in explaining that to you when you'll be dead in less than twenty-four hours," she said. Black smoke drifted around her, and she disappeared.

I stared at the place she had stood and shoved my hands in my pockets. Things just got a whole lot more complicated.

TWELVE

I needed to know who Swift was. She had enemies that made mine look friendly, and that was not an easy feat. Besides, she had read my file; it was only fair that I read hers.

Records that weren't available in the System were kept down in what the department fondly referred to as The Cave. It was in the back of the IMIB building, at the end of a narrow hallway; and for some reason, there was always a light out.

Sergeant Patrice Jackson was the woman to schmooze if you needed something. She was sweet as Southern apple pie if you treated her right, and vicious as a moccasin if you pissed her off. She liked me for reasons I'd never understood.

Her office was the barrier into the rooms that held the old paper files and evidence. There was no door on this side of things — I had no idea how she got in and out — just inch-thick, bulletproof glass and runes that'd smoke you if you tried to throw magic at her. Not that she couldn't beat you into a pile of mush on her own if she wanted to. There were rumors that some idiot had tried once, and that she kept his remains in a jar in her desk drawer.

"Patrice," I said with my most charming smile. "How are you today?"

Patrice wiped a stray smear of mustard from the corner of her mouth and gave me an unimpressed look. "Sugar, when are you going to stop trying to flirt with me to get what you want? You know it never works," she said with a thick drawl. Her black hair was going gray at the edges, but the laugh lines around her eyes and mouth kept her from looking stern.

"A man has to try," I said with a more genuine smile.

She snorted and leaned back in her chair, crossing her arms. "All right, what do you need?"

"Any information you have on Detective Lexi Swift, recently transferred from Magical Artifacts," I said.

Patrice tapped away at her keyboard as I drummed my fingers on the counter impatiently. She pursed her lips, her wrinkles deepening as she frowned. "What have you gotten yourself into?" she asked, eyes still locked on the screen.

"What do you mean?" I asked.

"This woman's file is locked down so tight you'd need Magister Level clearance to view it," Patrice said, twisting her monitor around so I could see it. Sure enough, everything was blacked out, and a password was required to view any information about Swift.

I ground my teeth together. "Thanks for trying, Patrice. I owe you a Coke," I said, pushing off the counter.

"You better bring me a bottle of Jack with that Coke the way you're always stressing me out," Patrice said, shooing me away. "Get out of here before you get me in trouble for trying to hack the system or something."

I snorted but left as instructed. None of this made any sense. If her history was such a big secret, what was she doing working as a detective?

Swift held out a cup of something hot. I sniffed and the distinctive scent of matcha filled my nose.

"Are you bribing me now?" I asked.

"It's a peace offering," Swift said, holding the cup out closer to me.

I snatched the hot tea and took a sip. It was perfect. She had remembered my order despite complaining about how complicated it was. What was she, some kind of stalker? I frowned; that didn't mean her secrets suddenly no longer mattered. "Should I send you my dry cleaning bill as well?" I asked, taking another long sip.

She narrowed her eyes. "Don't push your luck."

"Instead, maybe you can explain why I got a visit from a Shadow Mage last night when I was less than three blocks from home. In Kichijoji," I added for emphasis.

Swift froze. "What did she look like?"

"So you know it was a woman," I said, stepping in close, forcing Swift to back up into the wall. "Who is she, and why does she want you dead?"

"It's a long story," Swift said, her jaw tight. "I need to know what she looked like. Did she tell you her name?"

"You're not in any position to be making demands, Swift," I retorted. "You have yet to explain why any of these people are trying to kill you. They're following me around, threatening me. I have had my fair share of people trying to kill me, but at least I knew why they wanted me dead."

"What do you mean, threatening you? You aren't involved in this, she wouldn't have done that," Swift insisted.

"Then you obviously don't know her very well," I said, leaving out the part where I refused to stay out of things and let them kill her. I didn't want her getting the impression I cared about her or anything like that. It was just the principle of the thing; if you told me to back off, I doubled down.

"Blackwell, Swift," Bradley shouted down the hall. "Get in here and give me an update, and it better be a good one. I just got off the phone with the mayor and he's pissed. Apparently his wife's cousin was the poor idiot that had his arm ripped off by the werewolf."

I immediately turned and headed toward Bradley's office, leaving Swift to follow or continue glaring at me.

I walked through the door to Bradley's office, and he gave me a suspicious look. "Blackwell, why the hell is your hair pink?"

"Team bonding exercise," I ground out, irritated with Swift all over again. She had been nothing but trouble so far.

THIRTEEN

"Billy," I said, placing my palms on the counter. He immediately began to sweat and hunched down over his keyboard, refusing to look at me. "I need a car."

"I'm sorry, Detective Blackwell, but we're...all out," Billy said with a surprising amount of determination in his voice. Dammit, now I'd feel bad giving the kid a hard time. I knew I intimidated him.

"What about me? Can I rent one?" Swift asked, stepping up and smiling at him from under her lashes. I had almost forgotten how hot she was until she did something like that.

A blush crept up Billy's neck, but he shook his head resolutely. The kid had a will of iron. "Sorry, you're both banned."

I groaned in frustration. "How long this time?"

Billy shrugged. "I don't know, it's the fifth offense. It might be…"

"Don't say it," I warned, holding my hand up to stop him. It seemed like bad luck to say *permanent* out loud.

"Fifth offense?" Swift gritted out from between clenched teeth. "You've managed to destroy *five cars*?"

I glared at her. "I haven't destroyed a single car. *Criminals* have done all the damage."

"It's like you're a magnet for bad luck," Swift said combing her fingers through her hair to smooth it back from her face. "I can't believe I'm stuck with you."

Billy watched our back and forth, trying his best to hide his amusement. He failed.

"This conversation isn't over," I warned with a glare, as I shoved away from the counter, turning on my heel to storm off toward the Rune Rail. We didn't need a car while we were in Tokyo, but we would be in Seattle this afternoon; and I really didn't want to walk everywhere again.

Swift hurried to catch up, falling in step beside me. "It's not his fault, you know."

"I know, I just like to give him a hard time. He was timid as hell when I first met him; now he has a backbone," I explained as we jogged down the short flight of stairs to the platform. The Rune Rail wasn't like your typical subway system, obviously, and I still hadn't gotten over the awe it inspired.

Instead of a long underground track, the cars were spit out of a swirling, multi-colored portal – one you didn't want to touch unless you liked the idea of exploding. There was just too much magic involved for a body to handle. The center of the portal was conical, the magical field reaching out like a whirlpool. On the other end of the platform stood a similar, but opposite, portal. The magic stretched inward, ready to suck you into oblivion. Sometimes I was glad the Rune Rail cars didn't have windows.

"I don't think giving him a hard time about corporate decisions is really going to help him," Swift muttered, tapping her boot impatiently as she glanced at the screen that listed pending arrival times.

"Were you ever shy? Even as a kid?" I asked, leaning up against a nearby pillar.

Swift shrugged. "Not really," she acknowledged with a frown. "I spent a lot of time…" she paused, as if she realized she was about to give away too much, "in etiquette lessons. I learned how to speak to people, so there was no reason to be shy."

I chuckled. "Well, Billy didn't get that training. Giving him a hard time is basically a community service," I said, spreading my hands wide like the magnanimous person I was.

"You're delusional," Swift said, but she was smirking. Even if she didn't want to admit it, she knew I was right.

The portal twitched, then a brilliant light burst through the center as it opened. The sleek, black Rune Rail glided through, stopping soundlessly in front of us. Seams appeared around the doors, and they slid open underneath the flare of runes.

As I followed Swift onto the car, I thought I caught a glimpse of a white wing, but as soon as I looked, it was gone. The Valkyries never showed themselves unless there was a problem, other than little slips like that. I looked around, just in case, then stepped inside and sat down.

FOURTEEN

"I think it'll be best if I do most of the talking when we meet with my contact," I said.

Swift was immediately incensed. "I'm not going to muck up a simple conversation with a potential informant," she bit out.

"Nothing is ever simple with Hiroji," I muttered under my breath. "Look, it's just going to be a little complicated since he's been trying to kill me recently."

"Wait, he's been trying to kill you?" Swift demanded, halting in her tracks. "And we're going to see him? *In person?*"

"They haven't been very serious attempts," I said with a shrug. "It's more for appearances, or to annoy me. I haven't decided which. Knowing him, it's both. He's always been very practical that way."

"Exactly how long have you known this guy?" Swift asked, her brows knitting together.

"Since I was six years old, so about one hundred and fifty years, give or take a decade." I had stopped counting the years after I reach one hundred. Most mages did; after a while the exact number of years you had been alive just didn't seem to matter anymore.

Swift crossed her arms. "Are you telling me that the son, and heir-apparent, of a well-connected yakuza was your childhood best friend?"

"Yes," I nodded. "We had a falling out about twenty years ago; and once I joined IMIB, he started sending the assassins."

Swift ran her hands through her pink hair and took a deep breath. Her magical signature flared for just a moment, as if she were struggling to contain it. "This has to be against regulations in some way."

I rolled my eyes and kept walking. She was always so obsessed with the rules and regulations. I hadn't wanted to hear her nagging the first time, and I didn't want to hear it now.

"He's just another informant now," I argued. "We are not friends anymore."

"When you have a history with someone like that, they're never just a confidential informant," Swift muttered. She didn't press the issue any further though.

The yakuza had spread beyond the borders of Japan long ago. Moira had only helped that growth. In some places, their power rivaled that of the Mage's Guild, but Tokyo remained the heart of their organization.

One of the many legitimate businesses they used as a front for the more sinister operations loomed in front of us. The high rise was several hundred stories tall. Land was a valuable commodity in Japan; it was always cheaper and more practical to build straight up. They had the tallest buildings in the world now, though that title changed hands on an almost monthly basis, as people combined magic and engineering in an endless race of innovation.

Walking into the building sent a chill down my spine. I didn't really think he'd kill me, but there was always the chance. The Saito family was ruthless, and polite until they came for your head.

Hiroji and I had become friends by chance. We were both new students in a competitive school, and in that kind of place, you needed allies. We had each other's backs for a long time, but I had learned you could never really rely on someone.

The lower floors of the building bustled with oblivious office workers. Most of the people who worked there had no idea what the owners of the company were up to. Each sort of business was kept strictly separate.

Hiroji had been tasked with overseeing two or three of his father's businesses once he came of age. Eventually, he was put in charge of one of the more unsavory enterprises.

That had caused a hell of a fight. The old irritation made my jaw clench. I hated Hiroji's blind loyalty to his family.

We rode the elevator to the top floor in silence. Swift was stiff with disapproval, and my shoulders were tense with nerves despite my efforts to relax.

The elevator dinged on floor two hundred forty-six, and the stainless steel doors slid open to a spacious area. There were only four offices up here; a secretary sat in a glass-walled office outside of each door.

The top floor had plush, blood-red carpet complemented by light grey walls and a brilliant glass chandelier that hung from the vaulted ceiling. The space was an elegant mix of modern and traditional.

I doubted Hiroji had moved his office; he was just as particular as I was, and even less fond of change. Swift followed me toward the office to our left. The secretary rose as we approached and met us at the door to her office. She was dressed in a slim black suit with sedate heels. The picture of professionalism, unlike the woman in the red trench coat next to me.

"How may I help you?" the woman asked in perfect English.

"I'm here to see Hiroji Saito," I said with a short bow. "You can tell him it's Logan; I'm an old friend."

She returned my bow. "One moment, please." She hurried back to her desk and picked up the phone, turning away from us. The secretary spoke too softly for me to hear, but a moment after she hung up the phone the door to Hiroji's office swung open. He stood in the doorway, face inscrutable.

His jet black hair was styled perfectly, not a hair out of place. The suit he wore looked new, a custom piece with a glint of silver in the pinstripes. His dark eyes bore into my face as we stared at each other.

He didn't react to the pink abomination that used to be my hair, but I could sense the question hanging in the air. Ten years ago, he would have given me shit for weeks for something like this. Seeing him stare impassively from the doorway was another twist of the knife in my back. I had thought of him as my brother, but that was all in the past now.

Finally, he stepped back and motioned for us to join him. Swift marched forward without hesitation and I followed behind her.

"Bring us tea," Hiroji said to his secretary before closing the door behind us with a loud click that echoed through the large office.

The floors were some kind of light wood that was polished to a shine. The north and west walls of his office were glass. From this high, you could see most of Tokyo on a clear day. Unfortunately, it was overcast. The building was shrouded in clouds, giving the room an ethereal vibe.

Hiroji strolled over to the window and looked out into the mist, slipping his hands into his pocket. "The last time I saw you, I told you if you ever set foot on any of my father's properties again, I would remove your head from your neck," he said, speaking in Japanese.

Swift stiffened, her fingers twitching as she prepared to summon her mace. I didn't think she spoke Japanese, but his tone was menacing.

I laughed. Hiroji's head snapped toward me, a frown tugging at his lips. "You were drunk and threw a still-full bottle of sake at my head that same night," I said, responding in Japanese. "Are you saying you actually meant it?"

A katana hung at Hiroji's hip. His blade was a more traditional sword, runed for durability, not to act as a focus like mine. He could draw it faster than anyone I knew, other than Master Hiko, our teacher.

I kept my eyes on his face, but all my attention was on the hands tucked in his pockets. If he so much as twitched toward that blade, only one of us would be walking out of here alive, and I couldn't say for sure it would be me.

“Are the two of you going to keep insulting each other in Japanese?” Swift asked, raising a brow. “If so, I can just leave.”

Hiroji snorted, breaking the tension crackling between us. “Apologies,” he said, reverting to English. He walked to his ornate desk and sat down. It was crafted from Australian Lacewood, a rare and expensive wood with an intricate grain of sharply contrasting red and gold lacy patterns.

"Please, have a seat," he said, gesturing at the two low-back chairs in front of us. We both complied, but the adrenaline pounding through my veins made me feel like I should still be on my feet.

"What do you want, Blackwell?" Hiroji prompted, his eyes straying from me to Swift. I didn't like him looking at her, though I didn't really want to examine all the reasons why right now. “I have a meeting in fifteen minutes, so this will have to be a brief conversation.”

"Martina Bianchi got a bit of a sunburn a couple of days ago," I said, watching his face for a reaction I knew I wouldn't get. They'd called him the Iceman in school. No one could get past his poker face unless he let them.

"More than a sunburn according to the news reports," Hiroji commented. There was a single knock at the door before it opened. The secretary walked in balancing a tray of tea on one hand. She carried it to the desk and filled three cups. After handing each of us our tea, she hurried out of the room. I took a sip, then cleared my throat and continued. "She was the matriarch of a well-established...family in the area," I said, dancing around the word mafia. There was too much history, and too many arguments, between us to use that word without starting another one.

"Yes, I was acquainted with Ms. Bianchi," Hiroji admitted, nodding his head. "Her death was unfortunate."

"Most murders are," I agreed.

Hiroji's eyes flicked up at that. "Has it officially been ruled a murder?" he asked.

"Yes," Swift said, leaning forward to set her empty cup on the desk. My cup was still almost too hot to drink. How had she downed it that fast without scalding her taste buds off? "She was possessed, and forced to kill herself. Blackwell suggested this visit because he thought you might have insights into who her business rivals might be." She crossed her hands in her lap, looking for all the world like a prim lady. I couldn't look at her face without seeing the pink smoke leaking from her eyes as the berserker rage took over. It was an unsettling contrast.

"I am not involved in Ms. Bianchi's business," Hiroji said, taking a drink of his tea. He watched Swift, and I could tell he was interested. He had always liked bold women, something his father had not approved of in the slightest.

"Yeah, we get it," I said, impatient to be out of here and done with this conversation. Coming here had been a mistake. "This isn't a fishing expedition to see what activities you have been involved in; we are simply looking to verify who had the most to gain from her death."

Swift frowned at me, but I pretended I didn't see it. "Have there been any recent power shifts? Mergers perhaps?" she asked, ever the diplomat.

Hiroji ignored me entirely and leaned forward to answer Swift's question. "Business in that area has been stable for some time. In fact, the only disruption has been Ms. Bianchi's death," he said, speaking in pointless riddles. We all knew what he meant; the words you hid behind didn't change the reality of what he dealt in.

"Did she have any rivals at all?" Swift asked.

Hiroji shrugged. "A few that I can think of. Castiglione, Sanchez, and perhaps Yakov, though he was more of a business partner. Perhaps you should talk to the vampires," Hiroji offered. "They tend to have more conflicts within their own ranks than anything else."

"When they kill someone, it tends to be a bloody affair, not possession," Swift stated. She leaned back in her chair slightly and crossed her legs. Hiroji's eyes flicked to her boots. Then her legs.

"If you think of anything else, feel free to let us know. You have my number," I said, rising from my chair. We had gotten what we came for, and if he knew anything else he wasn't sharing it with us.

Hiroji raised a brow, but stood as well. "It was lovely to meet you, Detective Swift," he said, extending his hand to her. She shook it firmly, bowing her head slightly as he did.

Hiroji escorted us to the door and opened it. As we walked through, he tapped my arm and nodded his head back to his office. "A word in private?"

"Give me a minute," I said to Swift before shutting the door behind me and facing Hiroji, who drew a quick rune to muffle our conversation.

"That text the other day, about cleaning up my trash, what did you mean?" Hiroji asked, switching back to Japanese for added privacy.

I raised a brow. "The assassins that you sent, the bad ones."

Hiroji's lips thinned. "I did not send them," he said. "If I ever sent someone to kill you, you wouldn't have a chance to complain about it. You'd just be dead."

Underneath the threats was a hint of concern. He was warning me. Someone else was targeting me, and I had no idea who, or why.

"How comforting," I said. "Thanks for the heads up."

"I'm surprised you're working with Swift," Hiroji said.

I shrugged. "Yeah, well, I wasn't given much choice."

"Right," Hiroji said as if he didn't believe me. "It's probably best if you leave now, I like to give the impression that I cooperate with the IMIB, but not too much."

I snorted and turned toward the door, feeling very much like I was missing some key piece of information. His comment about Swift...it meant more than he was letting on. It seemed like he had more to say but had decided against it at the last moment.

I opened the door and Swift took a breath of relief.

"Aww, were you worried?" I asked as we strode toward the elevator.

"Don't be ridiculous," she denied.

My phone rang, interrupting our heartfelt moment. The caller ID showed Rune Rentals, but only one person ever called me from that number.

"Blackwell," I said as I answered the call.

"Hey, Blackwell, it's Billy," he said excitedly, practically shouting into the receiver.

I held the phone away from my ear slightly. "Tell me you have good news," I responded eagerly.

"Well...that just depends on how you look at it," Billy said, sounding shifty all of a sudden.

"Billy, spit it out," I warned. That caught Swift's

attention, and she leaned in a little to listen. Billy was certainly talking loud enough for her to hear.

"I have a car for you, but...it was planned for demolition anyhow," Billy hedged.

"What the hell kind of car is it?" I demanded.

"Oops, I've gotta go, my shift is over. You can get the keys from George!" Billy said, hanging up abruptly.

I lowered the phone and glared at it.

FIFTEEN

I unlocked the new rental car and cringed at the high-pitched beep. My GTR was gone. Forever. And I was stuck with The Clunker. I could have lived with it if they had given me a soccer mom car, but what I got instead was something that they must have scraped out of a back lot just to punish me. It was a pale yellow El Camino. The piece of crap didn't know if it was a truck, or a car.

"I can't believe they gave you this car," Swift said.

"It's hideous—" "It's so cool," we said at the same time.

I glared at Swift. "Seriously? Cool? Look at it!" I said, pointing at the offensive yellow paint and the long, useless bed where a trunk should be.

"It's a classic!" Swift argued, her eyes snapping with barely contained magic. She had a temper that I was learning went from zero to a hundred in no time at all. "I've always wanted one."

I stared at her, too appalled for words. This car was an abomination. An insult to everything I held dear.

"Let me drive if you hate it so much," she said, sticking out her hand.

"No way," I said, marching toward the driver's side. "You're never getting to drive."

"Chauvinistic asshole," Swift muttered as she pulled open the passenger door and climbed in, slamming the door shut behind her. The leather seats creaked as she sat down.

"I'm not a chauvinist, though I am an asshole," I said, cranking the engine. It sounded anemic, and I knew this thing would end up lumbering around turns instead of hugging them like the GTR. "I wouldn't let you drive even if you were a guy."

"That doesn't make it better," Swift argued, throwing her hands in the air.

"Sure it does," I said, merging with the traffic. Thankfully, her contact was only a fifteen-minute drive away. I didn't think I could stand any longer than that in this thing. "I may be an ass, but I'm not actually a bad guy. There's a difference."

"The only difference is—"

Her words were cut off as an SUV rammed the back of the car. We spun out into the intersection and I tried to steer away from oncoming traffic, but another car clipped the front bumper. The force of the impact whipped us around for a third time. My shoulder hit the glass hard, and my teeth bit into my cheek.

I slammed on the brakes and we skidded to a halt. Pink magic glowed around Swift's hand as she began to summon her mace. She kicked her door open, sending it skidding across the asphalt before she jumped out into the street.

Smoke was pouring from under the hood, and, of course, my seatbelt was stuck. There was no way I was dying in this junker. I pulled the knife from my ankle holster and cut through it, ripping it free, then forced my door open and climbed out. But instead of stepping onto asphalt, I fell.

Darkness blurred my vision, and the oppressive cold of the shadow magic stole the breath from my lungs. There was not a single magic user more annoying than Shadow Mages. If you couldn't avoid the portals they created, there wasn't much you could do to counter them. And they were a bitch to catch up to if they fled.

I fought against the magic for a moment, but without being able to breathe or move, it was a losing battle. I had another option, but there was no telling what might happen if I used that. I'd just have to see what was at the other end of the rabbit hole.

SIXTEEN

Drip. Drip. Drip.

The noise made me want to rip my ears off. Heeled shoes tapped across the concrete floor and someone stopped in front of me.

"Quit pretending you're still unconscious," a familiar, threatening voice said. "I can sense that you're awake, idiot."

"Please tell me the car is totaled," I groaned as I forced my eyes open. I was tied to a chair in some sort of grimy, underground warehouse. The kind of place B-movie villains committed all their torture and ill-advised drug deals.

"The what?" the woman who had threatened me the night before asked, crossing her arms as she peered down at me.

"Yellow El Camino," I said, testing how tightly my

arms were bound. Very tightly was the answer. "There's no way you missed it."

The woman rolled her eyes. "I should have gagged you."

"Kinky," I said, winking at her. "My safe-word is potato." All my things lay in a pile behind her, including my katana, which sucked on several different levels. I didn't expect the bad guys to leave me armed, but they'd have been safer if I still had the sword; they just didn't know that yet.

The woman glanced at her watch. "You have about an hour left to live. Any last requests?"

"Let me go?" I asked. She looked at me, unimpressed, and I shrugged. "I had to try."

A sharp knock rapped against the door. She walked over, her heeled boots echoing off the concrete and metal. She cracked the door and began a quiet conversation with whoever was on the other side.

I craned my head over my shoulder, getting a look at the ropes around my arms and checking to see if they had Swift stashed in here somewhere. However, I was the only prisoner, which meant I was bait. Most likely for Swift.

There was no way to tell exactly how much time had passed, but I didn't think it had been long. My head felt fuzzy, but my shoulder was still sore from the wreck; and the inside of my cheek was still bleeding sluggishly.

"You're not getting out of those ropes, just in case you were going to waste your time trying. They're heavily enchanted," the woman commented as she walked back. The bald guy who had attacked Swift and me in the street trailed behind her. He sneered at me, but it was even less effective with the actually scary mage standing in front of him.

"So is this all some elaborate ploy to draw Swift in, then kill us both?" I asked, curling my hand into a fist. If I wanted to do this without dying – and I did, just for the record – then I needed a little time.

"It's fairly simple, actually," the woman said, her eyes flicking back to me. "We took you, and now Swift will come and attempt your rescue. We would have killed her on the street, but kidnapping you was much cleaner. We try to keep our disputes under wraps when we can. It's uncivil to make a scene in public."

"What exactly is your issue with her, by the way? That's always been a little unclear," I said. Maybe the bad guys would be honest with me about who she was and what she had done if no one else would. "Consider it my dying request," I added with a grin.

The woman pursed her lips, considering answering for a moment. "Lexi Swift is a thief and a disgrace to her family name. I'll consider it an honor to take her head."

Well, that was something. I had a hard time imagining her stealing anything with her aggressive belief in following the rules though. "A thief, huh? What did she steal exactly?"

"Definitely should have gagged you," the woman muttered, turning away and pulling out her phone.

If I wasn't going to get anything else useful out of her, then it was time for me to bust out of here.

I kept my magical energy tightly under wraps. When people felt it, I always got an odd reaction. Some people thought I felt pathetically weak, normally a sign they were weak themselves, or they felt the full depth of my energy and freaked out. I wasn't all-powerful. In reality, I was weaker than most mages, but only because I couldn't use the magic I had. It was too dangerous, except for situations like this where it was either die, or die trying.

SEVENTEEN

My fists shook as I reached into that dark part of myself that I normally tried to pretend didn't exist.

After my parents' murders, I had been on the verge of going completely insane. Master Hiko took me under his wing and gave me a chance. That chance was the katana. It suppressed my magic enough that I could focus it and actually use it without risking death.

Over the years my Master had made me practice without the katana, but I hated it. I liked being in control. I liked getting my way. The magic didn't care. All it wanted was mayhem.

"When are you expecting Swift to show up?" I asked, some of the strain showing in my voice. I just wanted to get enough energy in my hand to blast these ropes off my arms. The trick was do that without blasting off my actual arms.

"Don't worry. Your girlfriend will be here any minute now," Baldy sneered. "She can watch you die first."

"Rude, it's always ladies first," I retorted, digging my nails into my palm as the shaking traveled up my arms. "Besides, she is definitely *not* my girlfriend. I like women with a little more class."

The door flew open, skidding across the floor with Swift perched on top like a skateboard.

"You're one to talk, Blackwell," Swift shouted, pointing her mace at me. Her eyes glowed fiercely, and her magical signature flared out of her like a warning. I was resentfully impressed. She had also arrived about thirty seconds too late.

"Hey Swift," I shouted back.

"What?" she snapped.

"Run," I growled out. Behind me, the mayhem magic flared out, popping like a gunshot. The ropes melted away like ice cream on a hot day in Texas, but it didn't stop. Of course not. That would have been too easy.

I snapped my arms forward and the chaotic energy flew over me, smashing down in the place where the female mage had stood. The concrete crumbled into a crater of dust about three meters wide. A whisper of a shadow formed to my left. I jerked back and slung the magic there instead, but the Shadow Mage was already gone again. She was obnoxiously speedy.

"What the hell are you doing?" Swift demanded, locked in a struggle with Baldy.

"I can't hold this back much longer, just run!" I yelled back, turning in a slow circle. The magic I was born with was unruly, and almost uncontrollable. And now that I had let it loose, there was no turning back.

The Shadow Mage hadn't fled; I could still feel her like a bad sunburn. The heat of her magic hovered at the edge of my senses.

I felt a rush of air at my back and ducked just in time for a blast of cold energy to fly over my head. I shoved my arm back, and the mayhem magic surged toward the Shadow Mage, following her into her portal. I guess it was time to find out what happened when those magics collided.

Swift kicked Baldy with a shout. He tripped over his own feet and fell on his back. She brought her mace down on his head, and that, folks, was that. She really seemed to have a thing with smashing in heads. I made a mental note to not piss her off so often.

A twisting shadow tore the air itself apart, then hovered there, twitching. "Swift, I think we really need to run," I said, taking a step back. The magic shuddered in response to whatever was happening inside that portal. "Now!" I shouted, turning and running toward her.

Swift's eyes went wide, and she finally took my warning seriously. She sprinted toward the door as well. I slid to a halt, snatched up my katana, then chased after her.

The air split open behind me, and the Shadow Mage reached out of the portal. Black lines crawled up her face as the crazed energy consumed her. She shrieked, her hand outstretched as if we might save her.

Her torso dropped free of the portal, trailing guts and blood behind her. It had cut her in half. The magic ballooned out, swallowing up her remains, and then exploded.

Swift leapt through the doorway as the blast forced me through right after her. I wrapped one arm around her waist, lifted my katana like a shield, and smacked my palm against the rune on the pommel. Magic flared from it, and a bright, blue shield wrapped around us as we were engulfed in the mayhem magic.

EIGHTEEN

Encased in the shield we were safe, but it sure as hell didn't feel safe. The force of the blast launched us through the air. Rubble and dust flew around us, making it impossible to see. A chunk of concrete the size of a bus hit us from above. We smashed into the ground, trapped beneath it.

"What was that?" Swift asked, breathless. My shield was still active but was starting to crack. "I've never seen a mage destroy an entire building with one spell before." Her glowing eyes blinked awfully close to my face. I pushed myself off her, but my back hit the shield.

"After getting kidnapped and nearly killed, I think it's time you answered my questions," I said with a glare. This had gone on long enough. Either she would answer, or Bradley and I were going to have a long –

possibly violent – chat. Honestly, I still didn't want Swift as my partner so I would likely have that chat anyway.

She crossed her arms between us, jabbing her elbow into my still sore ribs in the process. "Chief Bradley instructed me to—"

"Stop citing the rules, and stop trying to blame this on Bradley. You just don't want to tell me," I snapped. My eyes were adjusting to the darkness, and I could see that she looked just as angry as I felt.

She ground her teeth together. "My family is trying to kill me," Swift said finally. "I've been disavowed, which is almost like being disowned, but it comes with a price on your head."

I groaned and rolled to the side, forcing her to scoot over so I could lie down and be trapped in a more comfortable position. I wasn't sure how much longer my shield would hold the rubble above us, but I figured that could wait until I got some answers. "And who, exactly, is your family?"

"They're with the Mage's Guild," she muttered.

The Mage's Guild ruled over all supernaturals, and they still do; but since the Magical Revolution, they had attempted to work with prosaic governments instead of outside of them.

"Which sect?" I demanded.

"It doesn't matter," Swift said. Magic glowed around her hand and she shifted a little farther away from me.

"Wait, what are you doing?" I asked. Surely she wouldn't.

"Getting out of here," she said, before punching straight through my cracked shield and the concrete that lay over us.

Like I said, crazy.

The slab of concrete cracked, dust falling from it. She punched it again, then planted both hands on it, and pushed. It creaked and lifted as she sat up. Berserker Mages had ridiculous levels of strength. I wasn't sure if I should be turned on or scared, but I was edging toward scared.

She gritted her teeth, and the bright magic flared from her eyes and hands. With a shout, she stood and threw the massive pylon off us.

I climbed to my feet, my jaw dropping as I took in the crater behind us. The bits of the building that had survived the blast were strewn in every direction. Most of it had been turned to dust though. Luckily, the warehouse was surrounded by a large parking lot. If this had been in the city...well...it was better not to think about the alternative.

I clambered on top of the concrete Swift had tossed off us and stared down into the blast zone. The crater was at least nine meters deep. I tightened my hold on the katana. This was why I didn't like using the mayhem magic without it.

"I'm so getting fired for this," I said, looking out over the devastation.

"You're lucky I haven't fired you on the spot!" Bradley roared, pacing in front of us. "You were supposed to keep him in line, not drag him into *more trouble*!" His face was so red it was verging on purple. He had to stop and breathe at some point or he was going to just pass out. "The Mayor's office called me *twice* about this latest incident, and I can't even sell it as for the greater good. *This is just a cluster fuck!*"

So maybe he didn't need to breathe after all. I crossed my ankle over my knee and settled in for a long-winded ass chewing. When Bradley got started like this, there was no point in arguing or reasoning with the man, you just had to let him vent. Loudly.

Swift was stiff beside me, apparently taking the rant to heart. I snorted, internally, of course. She was too attached to the rules. I had broken them so often I was immune to any sort of guilt trip. I could understand why she might feel guilty though; after all, this was completely her fault.

"Blackwell! Are you even listening?" Bradley shouted, jabbing his finger in my face.

"Of course, sir," I said hastily. I had definitely not

been listening, but I could guess what he had said. "And you have my word it won't happen again. I'm making it my New Year's resolution not to destroy any more buildings."

Bradley's cheeks puffed out as he attempted to contain whatever tirade he wanted to rain down on me. "You...irresponsible....undeserving...cocky... arrogant...*asswipe*!" He exploded on the last word, slinging his arms wide. *"It's not even January!"*

"Regardless, Swift and I have to go. We are late for an appointment with a special contact concerning the case," I said, yanking Swift to her feet with me. "We'll get you an update first thing tomorrow morning, and it will be good news." I shoved her toward the door and gave Bradley a thumbs up.

"It damn well better be, Blackwell, or I'll have your head stuffed and mounted on my desk!" Bradley shouted after us.

NINETEEN

Dust. Old Paper. And bergamot. I breathed in the strangely pleasant combination of smells and followed Swift into Gresham Rare Books. The front desk was manned by an old woman who sat suspiciously still. I paused, considering whether I should check to see if she was still alive, but Swift yanked on my arm.

"Stop gawking; we don't have time," she whispered.

"I wasn't gawking. She's not even my type," I insisted.

"So what is your type? Young and busty?" Swift mocked.

"Who are we meeting again?" I deflected. I did not want to go down that rabbit trail.

The front of the store was dimly lit, with shelves of books neatly arranged. Swift walked past all that and pushed open the Employees Only door. We walked through and my jaw dropped.

This was some kind of book mecca. The building stretched up at least eight stories high and was filled with a maze of books. In between the shelves, were stacks of even more books. A ladder rolled toward us, and a man with a shock of unruly white hair over bushy brows and thick glasses appeared.

"Lexi?" His thin lips curled up into a smile I could only describe as fond. "Darling, it's been over a month," he said in a posh British accent. "I was starting to wonder if you'd forgotten about me."

Swift grinned and hurried forward. He slid down the ladder, rather spry for someone who looked as old as he did, and caught her in a hug.

"Professor Gresham," Swift said, returning his hug with enthusiasm. "I'm sorry it's been so long. Things have been a bit…unfortunate lately. I'm sure you heard."

He tilted his head in sympathy. "Of course, yes. Even I couldn't miss that sort of news. Who is this with you?" Gresham asked, turning his owlish eyes to me.

"Detective Blackwell, my new partner," Swift said, her tone odd. Gresham tensed slightly, like my name meant something to him. Something unpleasant.

"Really?" he asked.

"Yep," Swift said, taking a step back. "We're actually here on business. We have a case that has all the signs of a possession but without anything that would indicate a demon is involved."

"Every victim, so far, has been a supernatural as well, a vampire and a werewolf," I added.

"Non-demonic possession of supernaturals?" Gresham asked, his face splitting into a grin once again. "I have plenty of information on the subject. Just follow me." He hurried into the stacks with Swift hot on his heels.

I followed as well, but hung back. The man had seemed to recognize me, but since I had no idea who he was, the thought was unsettling. This store was unsettling as well. The amount of magic packed in here was strange. If it was just books, where was it all coming from? It wasn't from the old guy.

A strange thump startled me. I took a step back and looked down one of the aisles we had just passed. A book lay on the ground, but there was no one around. I crept toward it, my senses focused on spotting whoever had knocked it down, but other than Gresham and Swift, the place was silent.

I stepped over the book and peered into the gap it had left. The shelf was solid behind it, so there was no way it was pushed through from the other side. Something nudged my foot and I bit down on a yelp as I jumped back, accidentally stomping on the book.

It twitched and the pages fluttered…unhappily. I mentally slapped myself. Books didn't have feelings. They were paper and ink, nothing else.

The book sighed and flopped open. I crouched down, careful not to touch it, and read the entry. It was something about the formation of the Guild of the Mages, a supernatural council that once ruled over all mages. It now heavily influenced the combined human and supernatural governments.

The book shimmied toward me. "You're very pushy," I said, picking it up with some trepidation. Nothing shocked me or leapt out at me. For whatever reason, the book just wanted to be read. Tucking my finger between the pages to save my spot, I closed the book and looked at the spine, it read: *A History of Magic: Fifty-Ninth Edition*.

"There you are," Gresham said from the end of the aisle. "I was momentarily concerned we had lost you."

"Sorry, it…fell," I said, waving the book at him.

"If you don't mind coming with me, Lexi and I think we've found something important," Gresham said, unconcerned with whatever the book had been doing.

I met him at the end of the aisle and followed him further into the maze of books. He led me up one flight of stairs, then another. I hadn't spent much time in libraries, much less a magical one.

"How long have you known Swift?" I asked, unable to bring myself to call her Lexi. It felt affectionate after the way Gresham said it. I didn't want anyone's mind to go down that line of thinking.

"Since she was born I think," he said. "I first remember her coming into the store regularly when she was around six or seven. She was a curious little thing, always asking questions and begging her parents for books."

"Were her parents book dealers or something?" I asked. Finally, someone with information I didn't need a high-security clearance to probe for answers.

"No, do you really not know? They're—"

"Professor!" Swift said, jogging toward us with a book in hand. "I think I've found our answer."

He hurried toward her, taking the book. I looked over his shoulder. The entry was on kitsune.

"Kitsune? Do those even exist?" I asked, looking up at Swift.

"Of course they do," she said. "They're not common, thankfully, but they've always been around. They are born with a single tail, gaining more through acts of heroism, or simply old age. They can possess a person, though they struggle to control them the purer their heart is."

"And they can possess a supernatural?" I asked.

Swift nodded, a strand of her bright pink hair swinging over her eyes. "Look at the section on cravings," she said, pointing at a paragraph on the right page.

I skimmed the entry. Apparently, their victims often had strange cravings for red bean paste and onigiri.

"That would explain the onigiri we found in the werewolf's apartment and the vampire begging us for food," I said. Thank Merlin, if this was what we were looking for, I was one step closer to solving the case and getting rid of this hideous pink hair.

"The kitsune has a ball worn on a collar around its neck," Swift said, pointing to the next passage. "If that ball is stolen, or the kitsune is tricked into giving it up, then whoever has the ball can control it."

"If one of Martina Bianchi's rivals managed to do that, it could explain the murders," I said, as I skimmed the rest of the page.

"I'll take this one," Swift said. "And the other on Japanese mythology."

"Did you find the last one on the list?" Gresham asked.

"No, and I'm also missing number six," Swift said, pointing at a scrap of paper that Gresham must have hastily scrawled the list on.

"That one should be up there," Gresham said, pointing overhead. "I'll find the other. It may have been put up on the wrong shelf."

Swift climbed back up the ladder searching for one book, while Gresham headed into the maze of bookshelves for another. I followed him, still needing an answer to my question.

Once we were out of earshot, I jogged to catch up to

Gresham. "It seemed like you recognized my name when Swift introduced me."

Gresham paused near the end of the row and squinted at a particularly faded book. He avoided my gaze and pulled a book from the shelf. "Hmm, I'm not sure what you mean," he said, thumbing through a book with an absent air. "Ah, yes, this is the one." He brushed past me and hurried back down the narrow aisle.

I resisted the urge to kick the bookshelf and trailed after him. Somehow, Swift had warned him of telling me anything about her.

When I got back to them, Swift had a stack of books. "Thanks again, Professor," she said with a pleased smile. "This is exactly what we needed."

Gresham nodded and scooped up the books. "Follow me," he said cheerfully.

Swift was silent as we walked, lost in thought. We exited through the same Employees Only door into the store front. The old woman was still asleep, or dead, at the counter. She didn't so much as twitch as Gresham slapped the books down and rang up the purchase for Swift. For some reason I had expected them to be free, but this wasn't a library.

"Are you buying that one as well?" Gresham asked, pointing at the book still in my hand.

I looked down in surprise. I had forgotten I was even holding it. Maybe the book was enchanted with a little something I hadn't noticed. I was a lot of things, but I wasn't normally absent-minded.

"Oh, I wasn't planning on it," I said, frowning at the book. "It just fell off a shelf as I walked by, then flipped itself open when I went to put it up."

"Ah, yes," Gresham said. "The store is enchanted to help you find the answers you most urgently need. If the book chose you, then you need it."

"Are you sure this is wise?" Swift asked Gresham quietly.

"Of course it is. Knowledge is power, and the truth will set you free, or however it goes," Gresham said, waving his hand at Swift dismissively. She eyed the book as if it might bite her, while he tapped at the old-fashioned till happily. "That'll be two hundred fifty dollars, please."

I snapped my head up. "What? That's ridiculous for a book."

Gresham pressed his thin lips together in disapproval. "Without the family and friends discount, it would be three hundred and eighty dollars," he said, his accent making him appear every inch the disappointed professor.

The book shivered, practically begging me to buy it. I sighed and dug my card out of my wallet, sliding it across the counter. "This book better be great," I muttered.

TWENTY

I groaned and rolled over, slapping off my alarm clock. It was 11:00 p.m. in Kichijoji, and that meant it was morning in Seattle. My schedule at IMIB consisted of "get your cases closed", so I set my own hours. Unfortunately, that meant getting up in the middle of the night after four hours of sleep to go back to Seattle.

I tapped the button that controlled the shades, and they rolled back from the glass windows that stretched the entire length of the studio apartment. I could have afforded a bigger place, but this unit had the best view. The lights of the sprawling city stretched into the distance. Tokyo was always bright, even at night.

My feet padded soundlessly across the tatami mats as I walked over to the closet. My suits hung in a neat, black row. Directly underneath, my watches were laid out on a backlit shelf that lit up as I stopped in front of it. It was orderly, unlike the rest of my life.

Even as tired as I was, I had slept fitfully. The strange inconsistencies in the case weighed on my mind. If someone had managed to steal a kitsune's ball, how had they done it? They had to be insanely smart, or strong. But if they were strong, why not just rob the stores themselves? They had gone to a lot of trouble to rob these places, then they made it obvious that the people had been possessed by having them act completely out of character. I was sure the werewolf would have been forced to kill himself, as well, if Swift hadn't done it while trying to stop him.

I tugged on my suit jacket and stepped in front of the mirror to put on my tie. The damn thing always ended up crooked if I wasn't watching as I tied it. I hated it and thought it was a liability during a fight, but IMIB required it for all officers. At least I didn't have to wear a uniform.

Paper crinkled behind me. I groaned in irritation. That book had been flipping itself open all night. Every time I shut it, it opened right back up. I thought whatever irritating magic had caused it to act up was connected to the bookstore, but either it was part of the book itself, or the spell somehow hadn't been satisfied yet.

It fluttered again when I turned to look at it as

though it could sense me. Giving in, I walked over and picked it up. It was open to the same section I had read in the bookstore, but the pages were quivering in anticipation.

I ran my finger down the crisp parchment and read the passage again. It droned on about the formation of the Mage's Guild and the families who had founded it: Larkspur, Zhang, and Weber. Blah, blah, blah...my finger paused on the page as I reread the next paragraph.

The three Founding Families have split off over the years. Many descendants of the Larkspur family are still heavily involved in the guild; however, the most direct descendant would be Sir Malcolm Swift, the current Lord High Chancellor of Mages.

I was an idiot. That was the only explanation. Swift was a fairly common name, but the top-secret files, the assassination attempts, and the weird lies should have triggered something in my mind to connect the dots.

Lexi Swift was the daughter of one of the most powerful families in the entire world. And her parents were trying to kill her. But why? What could she have stolen that was so important?

I lowered the book, but the pages flipped again. Irritated, I lifted it back up. The passage made my blood run cold.

On May 9, 1880, the day the Mage's War ended, esteemed magical researchers, Linda and Howard Blackwell, were trag-

ically killed on the very same day. The nature of the incident sparked rumors and accusations of murder, but no clear suspect or motive has ever been discovered. Their sole heir, Logan Blackwell, has sworn to investigate their deaths on his own.

TWENTY-ONE

My phone buzzed with yet another text from Swift, probably asking where I was again. I ignored it and knocked once on Chief Bradley's door before opening it and walking inside without waiting for a response. Two detectives looked up from their conversation with the Chief. The surprise fell from their faces as soon as they saw who had interrupted their meeting.

"Out," I said, jabbing my thumb at the door.

They sighed and stood, long used to my antics at this point. Chief Bradley simply leaned back in his chair and picked up his cup of coffee. I waited until they walked past and the door clicked shut behind me.

"Swift. Daughter of the Lord Chancellor of the Mage's Guild," I said, my voice rising in volume with each word. "Care to explain how she ended up working for the IMIB? And as my partner?"

"No," Bradley said, lifting the cup to his mouth and taking a sip.

I ground my teeth together in irritation. He knew way more than he was letting on, which seemed to be a trend. Everyone knew more about what was going on than I did lately. I didn't like it. "Did you know her parents are trying to kill her?" I demanded.

Bradley scoffed. "That sounds a bit far-fetched. I'm sure the Lord Chancellor has better things to do. Besides, the Mage's Guild no longer carries out political assassinations. Everyone knows that."

Everyone knew the opposite, actually; it was just something you never said out loud. Bradley calmly looked at me over his cup, trying to communicate that very thing telepathically, judging by the twitching of his mustache.

There were a thousand questions on the tip of my tongue, none of which I could ask here. Whatever was going on, Bradley knew about it and was involved somehow. I didn't think he was trying to kill Swift, but he might be protecting her. The Chief wasn't a saint, but he had been known to stick his neck out for people when he thought it was the right thing to do.

I dragged my hand down my face. "You should have told me who she was from the start."

Bradley scoffed at me. "You do better when I let you figure it out on your own."

"What's that supposed to mean?" I demanded.

"Means you have a problem with authority," Bradley said, shaking his head with a smirk.

That manipulative old badger. He had played me. I was pretty sure he had intended me to be an unofficial bodyguard for Swift, but he knew I'd have turned him down flat if he had ordered it.

He stood and drained his cup of coffee, then walked toward me and clapped his hand on my shoulder. "Now, I have another meeting. Don't interrupt this one." With a grip like iron, he steered me toward the door and shoved me out of his office.

I straightened my jacket and started toward my office when I felt something I hadn't felt in a long time. High-ranking officers in the Mage's Guild were required to broadcast their magical signature. It was something of a warning, and a courtesy. It used to give criminals a head start, just to be fair.

Pausing in front of my office door, I looked over my shoulder and saw a Magister, dressed in the traditional red robes, walking into Chief Bradley's office. Where Magisters went, trouble followed. I frowned and pushed my door open.

Swift sat stiffly in the chair farthest from the door, in

the only spot in the office not visible through the large window.

"They give you the creeps, too?" I asked, knowing full well that wasn't her issue.

"You could say that," Swift said, pressing her lips together in a wan imitation of a smile.

Swift yawned, covering her mouth primly. I stepped through the hole the vampire had punched in the side of the bank and scanned the area. There was no residual magic, so it was unlikely any spells were cast to aid the vampire when she robbed the bank.

I turned back to ask Swift a question, but she was yawning again. "Merlin, just get some coffee. Did you not sleep at all last night?" I asked.

"I was re-reading the case files and lost track of time," she said, waving her hand at me dismissively. "Have you found anything new, or did you drag me out here for no reason?"

Whenever I got stuck on a case, I always went back to the beginning. I needed to go to the scene of the original robbery again and look through the place, hopefully, without an interruption this time.

"If this was a rival striking back, there are easier ways to do it than having something possess the victims and force them to rob a bank before committing suicide," I commented, even spelling it out like that took too much effort. "Even easier ways to kill her."

"Easier isn't always better. Maybe they were trying to make a spectacle of it. They certainly did whether that was the point or not." Swift crouched in front of one of the lockboxes and examined it. Grabbing a glove from her pocket, she tugged it open. She looked back with a raised brow. "Didn't they say nothing had been taken except for cash?"

"They did," I acknowledged, crouching beside her. She tried a few more around that lockbox, but the others were still secure. "What's the number on it?"

Swift wiped the dust off the front so she could read it. "Three-nine-four."

I pulled out the list the bank manager had given us with the names registered to each lockbox and searched for that number. The owner of this lockbox was Frank Castiglione.

"Sounds like we have a new person to question," I said, showing her the name.

TWENTY-TWO

We had been downgraded from the El Camino, which had been totaled – and, yes, I had celebrated – to some tiny European car that I could barely squeeze into. I wasn't exactly a giant, but at one hundred and eighty centimeters tall, I required a car that wasn't intended for ants.

I climbed out, stretching my sore back. "I'm going to have to bribe Billy to get me a decent car again," I grumbled.

"You're going to get Billy fired if you destroy another car," Swift said, her brows pinching together in disapproval. "You should request one of the standard issue sedans that are runed for sturdiness."

I gave her an appalled look. "Where's the fun in that?"

She rolled her eyes and muttered something under her breath. She did that often around me.

"I have a sudden craving for good food. Let's discuss what we have so far over dinner, in Tokyo," I suggested. My stomach was growling and I didn't get a chance to eat dinner there that often anymore. It would only take us thirty minutes to get there, at most, and we were already at the Rune Rail station; I saw no reason not to go.

"No, we need to get back to the office," Swift said, picking up her pace as if her comment reminded her to be in a rush.

"Even you have to eat," I said, exasperated. "Or do you starve yourself in favor of doing paperwork every day?"

"It's just a waste of time. We could eat and work at IMIB without wasting an hour getting some fancy dinner," Swift said, throwing her hands up in the air.

"I'll take that as a yes. Come on," I said, grabbing her by the elbow and dragging her toward the proper Rune Rail level.

She groaned in protest, but followed. "This better be amazing food," she grumbled.

"It'll be the best you ever had," I said, slinging my arm around her shoulders. She shrugged my arm off with a glare.

Swift followed me up the short steps that led into the restaurant. We were greeted at the door by a woman in traditional dress. Mizumi had been the hostess at the restaurant for as long as I had been coming there. She was aging gracefully but had faint lines around her eyes and mouth these days.

"Blackwell, welcome back," she greeted with a bow, speaking in Japanese. "Would you like your usual table?"

"Yes," I said, returning her bow. "My friend will be joining me today."

Mizumi inclined her head toward Swift, then led us through the restaurant. Whenever the weather permitted, I sat outside. The tables were arranged with a view of the garden and small creek that ran through it.

The stress of the week unwound as I sat, crossing my legs in front of me. The cadence of the water rushing over the rocks, the quiet chatter, and the scent of well-cooked food drifting on the breeze was my idea of heaven.

Swift knelt, then shifted her feet to the side, then swung them around and crossed her legs. She bumped her knee against the low table and rubbed it with a huff.

"I take it you don't visit Japan often?" I asked with a smirk.

She glowered at me and snatched up the menu. "I've

spent more time in Europe. Have you lived here long?" she asked.

"About fifty years or so, off and on," I said.

Swift skimmed the menu, pursing her lips as she tried to decipher the foreign letters. She slipped her phone out under the table, trying to shield it from my view, and tapped something in while glancing at the menu. Her fingers tightened on the leather-backed parchment, and her eye twitched. "Ten thousand yen. Is that a…typo?" she asked.

"No." I furrowed my brows. "That's for the chef's choice special, right?" I tugged at her menu to see which option she was looking at, then nodded. "It's great, you should try it."

"I'll just have tea or something," Swift said, setting her menu down and shoving it toward the edge of the table. She grabbed the book she had brought with her and stared down at it, but I didn't miss her stomach growling. Listening to it grumble for the whole meal would be distracting.

A waitress approached and knelt next to the table, then carefully set two small cups in front of each of us. Holding a towel under the spout of the teapot, she poured a perfectly equal amount of hot tea in each cup.

"What would you like to eat?" she asked in Japanese

"We'll both have the chef's choice," I responded with a light American accent I hadn't ever been able to get rid of. I spent too much time still speaking English to sound like a native Japanese speaker.

"Nothing for me," Swift said in English, speaking slowly in case the woman had a hard time understanding her.

The waitress looked at me, confused.

I shook my head. "She is confused, two meals, please."

The waitress smiled politely and rolled up onto her feet. I still had no idea how they managed to perform such an awkward movement so gracefully.

I hadn't considered cost when I brought Swift here. Anyone from an old family like hers should have plenty of money. She was as close to royalty as you could get in the mage world.

I was given a small trust fund when I turned thirty, but it had been my investments that had set me up for life. I had five times as much as I started with, not to mention a healthy monthly income from the interest alone. That wasn't even counting the inheritance I received after my parents were killed. My paycheck was a drop in the bucket. I lived modestly, other than my suits, watches, and fancy dinners. All right, so I didn't live modestly at all, but I tried not to flaunt the money.

She must have been given something similar, but since she had been disavowed, they must have taken it all away somehow.

"All right, so what we know is that these people have been possessed by a kitsune," I said, resting my elbows on the table. "But I've never heard of one killing people. At least not intentionally."

Swift shrugged her shoulders and flipped over another page. "Kitsune are tricksters. It makes sense for it to be robbing places, and in some ways the murders even make sense. They made a vampire walk out into the sun, and that werewolf was going to be next, most likely," Swift said.

"It didn't trick them; it forced them to kill themselves," I argued. "Kitsune are mischievous, not…evil."

"Maybe this one is different. It is odd for it to be possessing supernaturals," Swift said, flipping the book around and pointing at a picture of a snarling black fox titled *Nogitsune*. "Sometimes they go bad."

I pointed at a paragraph on the page next to it. "They can be controlled if their ball is stolen. Someone controlling the kitsune would explain all of this."

"Who is controlling it?" Swift asked.

"I have no idea. Yet," I said, pulling the book closer and flipping to something I had read earlier. "But it would have to be something smart, and most likely another supernatural."

"I still think it is a simple case of a kitsune that has gone evil," Swift said, crossing her arms.

The waitress appeared with a tray balanced on her

arm. She knelt and began arranging the various small dishes in front of us.

"Oh, I didn't order—"

I lifted my hand and cut her off. "My treat," I said.

Swift shifted uncomfortably, her shoulders inching up toward her ears. "You didn't have to do that."

"I know," I said, pausing our conversation to thank the waitress. "But I didn't want you trying to steal bites of my dinner when your hunger overwhelmed you."

Swift scoffed and stuffed a bite of beef in her mouth. She chewed quickly, not even taking the time to appreciate the flavor. "Whatever, Blackwell. Thanks for dinner."

I nodded and took a bite myself. The fish practically melted in my mouth. It had the perfect balance of flavor and simplicity. My eyes slipped shut as I chewed. I didn't scarf it down like a barbarian, unlike the person sitting across from me.

"Are you having sex with it, or eating it?" Swift asked.

I opened my eyes and saw that she was staring at me with a disgusted expression. "I appreciate my food," I said, unconcerned with her dislike of my eating habits.

"Apparently," she said, stuffing another overly large bite in her mouth.

I shook my head and took a sip of tea. "I think we need to refocus on the robberies. Someone must have scouted the places that were robbed beforehand. They needed to see it if they were going to use the kitsune to rob them."

Swift shook her head. "We can look at that angle, but we need to focus on how to find, and put down, a nogitsune in my opinion."

I tapped my fingers on the table. My hair was still hideously pink, but I was feeling arrogant. Besides, I *was* good at this, and now that I'd had some time to think about the case, I was sure I was right this time. "How about another wager," I offered. "If I'm right, you have to stop being such a pain in my ass about the rules."

"And if I'm right, I get to drive. Forever," Swift countered.

My fingers tightened around the chopsticks. This was a dangerous wager. "You're on, and you're going to lose this time," I said, thrusting out my hand. She shook it, and the magic flowed between us once again.

TWENTY-THREE

I toed off my shoes by the door and paused at the threshold. I'd known my master since I was a child. He had been going gray when we first met, but his hair was fully white now. He kept it buzzed short, but his neatly braided beard was long enough to tuck into the belt wrapped around his waist.

He stepped forward and swung the katana down in a sharp motion, ending the movement with a loud shout. He slid his foot around, eyes trained on invisible opponents. Two steps forward and a thrust, then he pulled the sword back and sheathed it.

Each step and movement were perfectly precise. He had been practicing this kata for longer than I'd been alive, and it showed. He was aware that I was here, but his perfectionist nature would not allow him to leave the kata unfinished. He had always told me it was disrespectful.

He sheathed the katana for a final time, then turned to face the mirrors. He knelt and laid the katana on the mat, sliding his hand down the sheath. He moved backward and bowed deeply, his head touching the floor. With the kata complete, he rose, picked up the sword, and finally turned to face me.

"I saw the news reports." He strolled toward me, putting the sword back at his waist. "I taught you better than that."

I stepped across the threshold and bowed deeply. "My apologies, Master Hiko."

His feet appeared in my line of vision and pain shot through my head as he rapped his knuckles against my skull. "Don't apologize, just stop losing control," he chastised. Also, didn't I teach you to never take your eyes off your opponent? You have grown weak."

"You're not my opponent," I said, as I rose from my bow and rubbed the top of my head.

"I taught you to be polite and courteous but also to have a plan to kill everyone. That includes me. Or did you forget?"

"I didn't forget. As for losing control, it was kind of intentional this time, and also not completely my fault."

He raised a bushy white brow. "Get your lies straight before you come here with excuses."

His leg struck out in a blinding move. I leapt backward just in time to dodge the attack. His katana flashed toward me; I drew my own sword and blocked the strike just inches from my face. The weapons are runed to be far more durable than prosaic weapons, allowing me to do things that would shatter a normal blade. We moved around the room, our swords flashing in a complicated dance.

Most students practiced with bokken, wooden swords, but Master Hiko had insisted that was a poor way to train. He also wouldn't let me use magic. The real risk of getting my head chopped off had lit a fire under my ass to learn quickly, and correctly. The kata had taken on a whole new importance as well. I assumed he had amazing control and wouldn't lop my head off. But I didn't exactly want to test that theory either.

"You can control your katana, but not your magic?" He followed up the question with a particularly vicious strike that made my arm shake. The shock waves of our runed katanas collided, kicking up a small cloud of dirt that sprayed outward with us as the epicenter. Maybe he really was trying to kill me.

"A Shadow Mage was trying to kill me," I said, countering and driving him back. "The mayhem magic was sucked into her portal, and the combination reacted unpleasantly. I was in control until then."

He scoffed and ducked under my swing, kicking me

square in the kidneys. "You were in control until you weren't. What a profound statement."

I gritted my teeth and blocked two fast strikes. He could always make me feel like an idiot, something no one else had ever managed, other than his wife.

"I just want to be rid of it," I snapped. He cut his katana at an unexpected angle. I parried the strike, but just barely. The sharp point sliced through my shirt and nicked the tender flesh of my stomach.

"Enough," he said, frowning at me and re-sheathing his sword, ending the sparring match. "You cannot be rid of it; therefore, you must learn to wield it. Work with it, not against it. How can you fight your enemies while you are fighting yourself?" He pointed at the blood seeping through my shirt.

I put the katana away. It was a crutch in many ways. It saved me from having to control the mayhem magic, and instead let me focus it. The problem came when I wasn't holding it.

He shook his head, disappointed in me. "Change your shirt, then we go drink. You are too melancholy tonight."

Master Hiko crept up to the open window. The room was dark and silent, but that didn't mean it was safe. He pressed his back against the side of the house and peeked inside. I stayed crouched down, ready to flee.

Quickly and silently, he whipped around and reached his hand inside. The keys clinked as his fingers closed around them. He paused, eyes searching the darkness fearfully, then slowly pulled his hand back.

Something whistled past and Master Hiko jerked back, practically falling into me. His hand was empty. The keys lay pinned to the dirt by a shuriken that had been thrown through the center of the keyring.

With tense shoulders, we turned back to the window. A slight Japanese woman with snowy white hair sat in the windowsill, one leg dangling over the edge, giving the appearance she was relaxed.

"Where are you going?" Sakura asked, tapping a shuriken against her thigh. Master Hiko's wife was a master of ninjutsu. I had begged her to teach me not long after Master Hiko took me under his wing. She gave me one lesson, then declared me too full of chaos to ever learn the way of the ninja. I had tried begging for a second chance, but she had just beat me up and sent me back to Master Hiko.

Master Hiko cringed backward. "Just to dinner," he said with a sly grin.

I would swear on my parents' graves she didn't move, but in the time it took me to blink, she was holding the shuriken underneath Master Hiko's nose. "You pass out drunk on the street again, and I will cut off your feet so you cannot go make trouble anymore," she threatened.

I stepped back, hoping to escape her notice, but she whirled around and pinned me down with a look. "You." She bit out the word with the kind of disapproval that Bradley wished he could muster every time I blew something up. "Should visit more often," she finished.

I bowed my head. "Work keeps me busy."

She scoffed angrily. "Not too busy to get into trouble."

I peeked up and gave her a cheeky smile. "Trouble has a way of finding me."

Her serious facade cracked and she smirked at me. "Go, drink, but make sure he takes a cab home. He is feeble and old and can't hold his liquor anymore," she said shooing us away.

Master Hiko grabbed his keys and tossed the shuriken back to her. She caught it with two fingers, then it disappeared somewhere in her clothes. The woman was scary. With one last warning glare, she walked back in the house.

"Let's hurry before she changes her mind," Master Hiko said, jogging over to his shed. A deep rumbling growl rattled the wooden structure, and he rolled out atop his custom Harley Hardtail.

I stepped into the shed and rolled out the motorcycle Master Hiko let me keep there, a small but nimble

Harley Sportster. It roared to life, and I followed my instructor out of his driveway.

The bar was only a few kilometers away, technically, but the winding mountain streets meant it was three times as far, in reality. The breeze was refreshing and distracted me from the stinging cut on my stomach. Master Hiko never allowed me to heal training injuries with magic. He didn't want the lesson to fade from my head too quickly.

I parked next to Master Hiko and pushed down the kickstand. Laughter and the smell of good food drifted out of the narrow alley that housed the town's izakayas. The one Master Hiko had been dragging me to since the day I was old enough to drink was tucked away between two taller buildings, but there was no way you could miss it. Lanterns were hung every few inches around the entire exterior and lit the place up like a beacon.

We claimed a small table wedged into the corner near a window. A few moments after we sat down, a bottle of sake and two small cups were placed between us, along with steaming bowls of Gyū-nikomi, beef tendon stew.

Master Hiko filled my cup with sake, then filled his own. "Kanpai!"

We both emptied the cups in one swallow. Master Hiko exhaled in satisfaction, threw his beard over his shoulder, and then dug into his soup. He had to keep it out of the way or it ended up in his food every time. It would be soaked in sake by the end of the night. I took a large bite of soup and groaned in appreciation; it never disappointed.

"What is the real reason you came to visit?" Master Hiko asked, watching my face carefully.

I picked up the sake and poured us another round, avoiding his question. He lifted his cup and we threw back the second shot.

"You make it sound like I never visit unless I want something," I said before stuffing another spoonful of delicious brothy beef into my mouth.

"Tch," he scoffed in irritation, "you never ask for anything, but lately you only show up when something is weighing on you. You come with questions. Spit them out so we can enjoy the evening and get drunk."

I hid my smile by looking down at the table. I guess I was more transparent than I realized. "I was assigned a partner at the IMIB, Detective Lexi Swift."

Master Hiko didn't flinch or react in any obvious way, but I knew him well enough to recognize the shadow that passed across his face meant something. He had heard her name before.

"Do you know her?" I asked, confused.

"No, why would I?" He filled our cups, then lifted his and waited for me to lift mine as well. Problem is, he *was* lying to me. I just had no clue why. He had never lied to me before. At least, that I knew of. He despised dishonesty.

I picked up my cup, and he toasted me with an enthusiastic kanpai. The sake burned down my throat. I refilled our glasses before he had a chance to take another bite.

"Some powerful people want her dead. The fight with the Shadow Mage that led to me blowing up that building was sent to kill her," I explained before drinking down the sake. The alcohol had begun to warm my cheeks, but we both still had a long way to go before we were drunk.

"Are you upset someone is trying to kill her, or annoyed you have been dragged into it?" Master Hiko asked.

"The assassination attempts are getting annoying, but what I was actually wondering is if her family was somehow connected to my parents' deaths," I said, watching Master Hiko's face intently. "They're part of the Mage's Guild, but I can't find much information on their role in the wars."

"I haven't associated with the Mage's Guild in centuries," Master Hiko said.

"I just thought you would remember the names of the major players," I said, rolling my empty cup on the table. He knew her name. The librarian was hiding something about her. And that book made it seem like they were connected to my parents. “Perhaps they’re connected to my parents' murders.”

“No one knows who was responsible for that.” Master Hiko snatched the cup out from under my fingers and filled it with sake. “To letting go of old worries,” he said, lifting his own cup. Sake sloshed over the rim and dribbled onto his fingers.

“To finding answers,” I replied.

“Perhaps the answers will find you when they are ready,” he said, an almost apologetic look in his eye. “Kanpai!”

I closed my eyes and threw back the shot. I wouldn’t get the truth out of him tonight, but I would eventually. I had to.

TWENTY-FOUR

Eight shots of sake later and my mood had only grown more bitter, while Hiko had turned into a freaking comedian. He balanced a chair on two legs and stood on the edge of the seat, his favorite drunk trick, and a sure sign it was time to cut him off.

He hopped down, catching the chair before it tipped over, and took a bow, which received boisterous applause. "Logan, you should see if you can cut off my beard," he said, pulling it from his belt and swinging it in front of me like I was a cat.

I stood and grabbed his shoulder. "I think it's time for you to take a cab home, or Sakura is going to get another phone call, and then all that's left of you will be the beard," I said quietly. Normally the dizziness that came with being drunk was part of the fun, but I found it annoying tonight. It wasn't dulling things like it usually did. My mind still felt painfully clear.

"Tch," Hiko scoffed. "When did you become my babysitter?" Despite his complaints, he grabbed his keys and tottered through the tightly packed tables to the bar. I watched until I was sure the bartender was calling him a cab before plopping back down in my seat and nursing another drink. Maybe I just hadn't had enough.

A shadow fell over my table and I tensed. Over the years, I had developed a sense of when I was being watched or followed, and when someone intended to do me harm. Very few people could skate under my mental radar, but there was one who had always managed it.

I looked up at Hiroji. He was out of his usual suit and in something slightly more casual, a button-up shirt and trendy jeans that probably cost more than the motorcycle sitting outside.

"You just missed Master Hiko," I said, waving in the direction of the door.

Hiroji pulled out the chair opposite me and sat down. He looked uncomfortable being in this old town. For me, it was always nostalgic, but I hadn't been disowned by my own master. That probably soured the memories a bit. "I know, tonight wasn't the time to see the old man again."

I flipped over a clean cup and filled it to the brim, then pushed it toward Hiroji. He picked up the cup and toasted me; we both drained them. I leaned back in my chair and waited for him to tell me why he was here. I hadn't seen him in over a year, so two meetings in two days had to be intentional.

"You shouldn't be working with Swift," Hiroji said, in a surprising display of bluntness.

I cocked my head to the side. "Why the hell do you care who my partner is?"

Hiroji picked up the sake and refilled our cups. "I meant it as a friendly warning. Surely you have figured out who she is by now, though I was surprised that you didn't know yesterday, so perhaps you have gotten slow in your old age."

I grabbed my cup, sloshing sake over my fingers before shooting it back without waiting for Hiroji. The table rattled as I slammed it back down. "A friendly warning? That's not really your style lately. I wouldn't think you'd care if I lived or died."

That got his attention. Hiroji ground his teeth together, and his nostrils flared. When we were kids, that look was always followed up by a punch. This time, he just turned away and twirled the cup between his fingers. "You think you're better than everyone else because you've chosen to bury yourself in a dead-end job that doesn't actually change anything." He looked up at me, resentment burning in his eyes. "You are not better than me."

I leaned forward slowly. "I am better than you for one simple reason. I have never killed, or hurt, anyone who didn't deserve it. You've sold out your principles for money, or your father's approval; I've never been able to decide which." My tone was calm, but I felt anything but. Hiroji pissed me off every time I had to talk to him since our falling out.

The cup cracked in Hiroji's hand. He calmly set the shards of pottery on the table and stood. "I can see warning you was a waste of time. Maybe you'll realize you should have listened while your spirit languishes in *Yomi.*"

He walked away, the fog of cigarette smoke closing behind him like a veil. Anger warred with guilt. I hated Hiroji for choosing to join the family business. I hated myself for not being able to talk him out of it.

If he was right about anything, it was that I hadn't been able to change anything that mattered in my time with the IMIB. We came in after the crime had already been committed. Sure, we punished the bad guys, but just for once, I'd like to stop them before they even got started.

I stood and walked toward the bar, intending to close out my tab, when I saw a woman slam her phone down on the table. Her thunderous expression reflected my mood perfectly.

The bartender looked up and nodded toward me. I

passed the pitcher to him. "A refill, please," I said in Japanese.

I leaned back against the bar and watched the woman for a moment. She wasn't dressed up, so she wasn't expecting a date. The tight jeans and dark-red blouse complimented her perfectly though.

She looked up and caught my eye. This was always the most telling moment. If she looked away, she either wasn't interested, or was too shy for me to bother. But she held my gaze.

The bartender nudged my elbow and handed me the sake. I turned back to the woman and lifted it in question. She pursed her lips, some of the anger melting into interest, then nodded.

I kept my eyes on her face as I walked over, watching her look me over. I stopped next to the chair across from her and set the sake on the table. "You look like you're having a shittier night than me," I said with a smirk.

"It's looking up, someone just brought me free alcohol," she said, reaching for the bottle. She poured two glasses and waved for me to sit down.

I didn't know, or really care, what her issues were, but I was sure she felt our connection, too. We saw the same thing in each other, the same need. Tonight we could help each other out – no strings attached, no messy emotions.

"Kanpai," she said, lifting her glass and leaning toward me. The light caught her green eyes, lighting them up like emeralds.

I tapped my glass to hers and felt the storm inside me begin to calm.

TWENTY-FIVE

The door rattled with the force of the pounding that echoed through my studio apartment. I jerked upright and rolled out of my bed, grabbing the katana on my way.

"What the hell?" My date from last night groaned and sat up. Her silky black hair was tangled from having my hands clenched in it.

"Stay in the bed," I said, stepping around the *shōji* wall divider and stalked toward the door. The pounding ceased, but there was a faint magical energy. I thought I had killed the mages that knew where I lived, but they could have told whomever they were working for. I glanced over my shoulder. Thankfully, my date had listened and stayed in bed.

The pounding on the door resumed. I walked toward it, my feet silent on the tatami mats. I held the katana with my right hand and reached for the door handle with my left, then cracked the door open.

"Swift, what—" I started as she stumbled toward me.

She slid down the door and collapsed. I swung the door wide open, catching her before she hit the floor and dragged her inside. I kicked the door shut with my foot. She groaned and tried to shove me away, but couldn't sit up.

"Oh my god she's bleeding!" my date screeched. She stood near the shōji door with the bed sheet clutched to her chest.

"Sorry I interrupted your date," Swift said, her teeth clenched tight from pain.

"It was already over." I pulled her hand away from the wound on her stomach and yanked her t-shirt up. A jagged, but shallow, wound stretched across her abdomen. The edges were tinged with green. With every beat of her heart, the sickly tinge spread slightly. The injury was made by a Bladeslinger. She was lucky it was just a slice.

Bladeslingers were mostly mercenaries. Much like she summoned a mace, they summoned blades. The magic on them created wounds that were slow to heal, even with magic, and more painful than any normal cut.

My date rushed past with her pants and shirt hastily pulled on. "I'll just go; don't worry about calling," she shouted over her shoulder as she raced out of the apartment, leaving the door wide open behind her.

"Guess you didn't make a good impression." Swift chuckled, but flinched as the movement jostled her wound.

I shook my head and rose to my feet, slamming the door shut. "Who attacked you this time? Another bounty hunter?" I demanded.

Swift glared at me from the floor. "Doesn't matter, I took care of it."

"You're too damn stubborn for your own good," I snapped before turning and stalking into the bathroom. I kept a first-aid kit in the cabinet above the toilet for emergencies. This kind of injury required magic to cleanse it, then bandages to cover it while it healed.

I grabbed the kit but paused in the doorway and took a deep breath before walking back out to tend to her. She got under my skin, and not in a fun way.

She had managed to crawl over to lean against the couch while I was in the bathroom. I knelt beside her and laid the kit on the cushion next to her head. Her normally sleek hair was streaked with dirt and blood. It hung in sticky tendrils around her face. A bruise was forming just below her eye on the curve of her cheek.

"Was it just one this time?" I asked, drawing a cleansing rune over the wound. Her stomach twitched as the warm magic sunk into her skin.

"I thought so, until the second one showed up and did this," Swift said, waving her hand at the wound.

I shook my head and drew two more of the runes above the length of the cut. As they linked together, the warm magic flared bright and hot. She hissed, but didn't flinch away.

"I would have thought you'd be experienced enough to watch out for a second attacker." The green tinge to her wound faded under the runes. I slashed through each to cancel them.

"I'll remember that next time," Swift snarked. Her breathing slowed, and she slumped in relief, reaching up to shove her hair out of her face. "Thanks, Blackwell," she said, her tone softer.

"Why'd you come here?" I asked, pulling out antibiotic ointment and a gauze bandage.

Swift stiffened at my question. "I didn't really have anywhere else to go, and I thought you would help me, since we're partners, and all," she said, jutting out her chin like I might argue.

"I wasn't trying to imply you shouldn't have come here," I said, pausing to look her in the eye and make sure she understood. I wouldn't have left her out there even if she'd been a stranger. "Just caught me by surprise. How'd you even get my address?"

"Your file, remember?" Swift said, grinning. A little

blood was still on her teeth from a punch she must have taken to the mouth.

"You've got a little..." I said, gesturing at my face while baring my teeth.

"Oh," she said self-consciously, bringing her hand up to hide her mouth. She sucked at her teeth trying to get it off.

I smeared some ointment on the bandage and laid it over the cut. Swift picked up the tape and tore a piece off. I took it and taped down each edge as she handed me three more lengths of tape.

"How did you manage to make it here with this injury?" I asked. Now that the shock of her arrival had worn off, it was a little odd.

She cleared her throat and shifted uncomfortably. "I was nearby."

I looked up at her face. "Are you stalking me now?"

"Just..." she waved her hand in the air, probably searching for an explanation that didn't sound insane. "I found a place in the area so I could make sure they left you alone."

I sighed, pinching the bridge of my nose. She was *guarding me.*

"Are you going to keep showing up on my doorstep in pieces?" I asked as I stood and walked to the kitchen. Swift pushed herself up unsteadily and sat down on the couch.

"I won't make the same mistake again," she said, resting her forearms on her knees.

"That's not what I meant," I said, irritated. I grabbed the electric kettle and filled it with water. "How long are they going to keep coming after you like this?"

"Until I give back what I stole," Swift said, staring at her hands.

I set the kettle down and braced my hands on the counter. "You stole something from the Mage's Guild, right?" I asked, my voice tight.

"Yes," Swift admitted tensely.

I turned around and she looked at me with a sheepish expression. "Why don't you just give it back?"

Swift swallowed and licked her lips uncomfortably. "I...destroyed what I stole."

I pinched the bridge of my nose between my thumb and forefinger and reminded myself to breathe. "Why would you do that?"

"It was an illegal magical artifact," Swift said, clenching her hands so tightly together that her knuckles had gone white. "They kept it even though they shouldn't have. The laws that ordered its destruction were created because those sorts of things shouldn't be used, but they found a reason to use it again. I couldn't let them."

"You should have just reported it to the police," I said, exasperated.

"I tried!" Swift said, anger flashing in her eyes. "But the rules don't apply to the rich and powerful, Blackwell, even though they should. I wasn't left with any other options."

The kettle began to whistle behind me. I turned and grabbed a glass teapot from the cabinet and measured two scoops of loose green tea into the strainer. I turned off the electric kettle and waited for the water to cool slightly before pouring it over the leaves. They unfurled and the light scent of tea filled my nose. It took only a couple of minutes to steep.

I grabbed two cups from the cabinet and poured some for both of us. "Here," I said, turning to Swift. "Have some tea while I make us breakfast."

Swift stood and accepted the cup. "I'm sorry you got dragged into this. I can ask for a transfer to a different department."

I scoffed and turned back to the stove. "Don't worry about it. No one else could handle your issues."

TWENTY-SIX

Swift grabbed her spare shirt from her desk drawer and hurried to the bathroom to change. The shirt I let her borrow hung off her like a dress. Sometimes I forgot how small she was because of the overwhelming amount of strength packed in her slim frame.

I dragged my hand down my face; stubble scratched at my palm. Apparently, I had forgotten to shave. Last night had been drama-filled, and this morning hadn't been any better.

Hiroji's warning hadn't shaken me as much as pissed me off, but it did raise more questions. Swift had finally told me some of the truth, though I suspected there was more to it. This was something I couldn't let go on forever though. She wouldn't survive the constant assassination attempts, and neither would my sanity.

I had adjusted the wards on my apartment to recognize her, insisting that if she ever needed back in she was welcome, and safe there. She had argued, but as per usual, I had ignored her and done it anyhow.

Chief Bradley opened the door to my office and walked inside without so much as a knock. I might barge into his every other day, but at least I knocked.

"Morning, Chief," I said.

"You look like hell," Bradley said, crossing his beefy arms and squinting at me.

"Late night followed by an early morning," I explained with a shrug. "What did you need, sir?"

"An update, progress, and hopefully a suspect," Bradley said, grabbing a chair and sitting down.

Swift walked back in, my shirt draped over her arm and her spare shirt hanging untucked over her pants. Bradley saw my shirt and raised a brow at me questioningly.

"Detective Swift's contact was able to confirm for us that this is an issue of possession, and that we're looking for a kitsune," I said, quickly trying to draw his attention elsewhere. "The issue is that someone is controlling the kitsune. We're planning on talking to Frank Castiglione–"

"Please tell me you are not dragging Castiglione in here for questioning. I do not need that kind of phone call from the mayor this early," Bradley huffed.

"His lockbox was emptied during the bank robbery,"

Swift interjected. "He's not a suspect, but he is involved. He might be another target."

Bradley leaned back, considering that. "If you have to talk to him, make sure it's a friendly conversation. He's about as connected as a prosaic can get, and prosaics are not fond of IMIB agents questioning their people."

"Understood," I agreed with a nod. "We'll go tonight, posing as customers. If I burn a little cash at one of his establishments, that should grease the wheels."

"I hope you mean your cash, and not anything out of my already anemic budget," Bradley grumbled, his mustache bristling in warning.

"Don't worry, this one's on me," I said, raising my hands in surrender. I had more than enough. If it made my life easier to spend it on something like this, I was all for it.

"I also want to talk to Alberto Bianchi in person," Swift interjected. "He's not a suspect currently," she said quickly when Bradley's hackles began to rise again, "but he could have some insight into who might have a grudge against his mother. I already contacted his secretary, and he's agreed to a meeting just after sunset."

I looked up sharply. She hadn't told me that.

"Make it happen," Bradley said with an aggrieved sigh before heaving his bulk out of the chair. "Swift, a word?"

She followed him outside without meeting my eyes. I

stayed in my seat, frustrated with the continued secrecy. It was pointless for them to keep leaving me out.

I grabbed my tablet and started pulling up information on Castiglione. If we were going to show up for a chat tonight, I needed to know where he liked to make an appearance.

After a few minutes, Swift walked back into the office. Whatever Bradley had said to her hadn't improved her mood any. She stood across from the System screen, hands on her hips, and scowled at it.

"When were you going to tell me about this meeting you set up with Bianchi?" I asked with feigned indifference.

Swift looked over her shoulder at me. "Right before I dragged you there."

"I'm not a fan of surprises," I said coldly.

Swift snorted. "Or of other people having opinions, especially if they differ from yours. You also don't seem to be a fan of teamwork either. Or basic manners."

"Next time, just tell me if you have some brilliant idea you have to see through," I said, trying to ignore the barbs of truth in her statement. Anthony Granger had beat those habits out of me, but after he had been killed...well, I didn't feel like putting up with anyone else.

"Sure thing, *partner,*" she said, crossing her arms and leaning back against her desk.

"It looks like Castiglione spends his Tuesday nights at one of his bars. There's a gambling den in the back; dressing nice is required," I said, gesturing at the dot on the map.

"All right," Swift said, crossing her arms. "What time should we show up? Eleven?"

"Yes, that will give us plenty of time to meet with Bianchi first." I leaned forward, looking at Swift consideringly. "You have any pretty dresses?" I asked with a grin. "Or should I get you one?"

Swift snorted. "Don't worry, Blackwell, I've got pretty dresses covered."

Partner or not, I was looking forward to that.

TWENTY-SEVEN

With the sun setting behind us, Swift knocked on the door to Alberto Bianchi's house. Well, one of them. This was his weekend home out in the suburbs. He spent the week in the city in a townhome not far from Pike Place Market.

The door opened, and a man in a cheap suit assessed us.

"Detective Swift, I have an appointment with Mr. Bianchi. This is my partner, Detective Blackwell," she said, nodding her head toward me.

"Badges," he said, his tone all business.

It appeared Alberto Bianchi kept a bodyguard. It wasn't uncommon for vampires that could afford it. After all, they were vulnerable as long as the sun was up, unless they were a couple hundred years old and well fed.

I pulled out my badge and pressed my thumb to the rune on the back. It flared green, confirming it was mine. Swift did the same.

The bodyguard stepped back and let us inside. The house seemed more suited to a soccer mom than a vampire with close ties to the mafia. It had vaulted ceilings, neutral walls, a beige couch, and that open layout everybody seemed to want these days.

Heels tapped down the hallway before being muted by the carpet in the living room. A short woman with long, straight, black hair that lay over her shoulders, kitten heels, and a bright-red pencil skirt appeared from around the corner.

"Detective Swift, Detective Blackwell, my name is Anna Johnson, I'm Mr. Bianchi's personal assistant," she said, stepping forward to shake Swift's hand, and mine. "I'm glad you could make it. Mr. Bianchi is on a phone call, but he should be finished in just a moment. Can I get you anything to drink? Water, coffee, a soda?" she offered with a smile.

I couldn't quite get a read on her age, and I suspected she might be a vampire, as well, based on the smooth way she walked.

"I'm fine, thank you for offering though," Swift said, sounding like a diplomat. She slipped into this professional way of speaking with practiced ease. Etiquette lessons my ass, she had spent time, and a lot of it, schmoozing people.

I simply shook my head and looked around the room. Something about this place bothered me a little. It seemed almost *too* perfect. Everything was arranged in just the right way to look innocuous, but no vampire really was, despite what they had led the prosaics to believe.

Those lies had been floating around ever since the Magical Revolution. Despite the name, it wasn't a war, though there was conflict. The prosaics didn't trust us. We were the dangerous creatures who stalked their nightmares. Abominations. Demons. Of course, once magic started making their lives easier, they got over that real fast.

Vampires and werewolves carried a stigma for longer than the rest of the supernaturals, but the Vampire Guild pushed forward with a very aggressive PR campaign that helped. Vampires became the savvy business managers with three hundred years' experience that everyone wanted to hire, or doctors that could smell an infection in the blood.

Likewise, werewolves became the soldiers whose wounds miraculously healed on the battlefield, fire-fighters that could bust through walls to rescue a trapped kitten, and friendly neighbors who always offered to let you borrow their tools. They were all about family, and what was more wholesome than that?

Prosaics knew we existed, but we still kept much of our nature hidden from them. Our laws came with harsher sentences than they could stomach. And vampires, well, there was nothing romantic about the way they fed.

Anna cocked her head as though she was listening carefully to something, then smiled. "Mr. Bianchi is done with his call and will see you now."

That answered the vampire question.

We followed her down the hall. Swift looked at the bare walls and frowned. Our eyes met for a second, and I could tell she was thinking the same thing I was. It didn't mean Alberto Bianchi was anything like his mother, but the place was creepy.

Anna opened the door to Alberto's study, without knocking, and ushered us inside. Alberto Bianchi looked to be in his early thirties, despite being about eighty years old. A goatee hid what otherwise would be a weak chin and helped make him look a little older.

He stood and smiled politely. "Detectives, I'm sorry I couldn't manage a meeting sooner, but with the...funeral arrangements, I've been unexpectedly busy," he said, stumbling over his words slightly. He shuffled some papers on his desk, presumably to hide his grief. However, like the rest of the house, that seemed like part of an act meant to hide his true nature. There was even a window behind him that provided a view of a perfectly manicured lawn. Most vampires avoided windows like, well, the sun.

"Thank you so much for taking the time to meet with us," Swift said, stepping forward. "The IMIB is doing everything it can to investigate your mother's murder. We do have a few questions, if you're up for it."

Alberto nodded and gestured toward the chairs in front of his desk. "Of course, anything I can do to help. My mother and I had our differences of opinion, but I expected her to live forever. This has been a shock."

"We'll start with the basics. Some of these questions we have to go over as a matter of routine, so please try not to take offense," Swift said, smiling warmly. She could put on one hell of an act when she wanted to. It was a little unnerving. "Where were you the night of your mother's murder?"

Alberto waved away her concern. "I completely understand. I'd be concerned if you *didn't* ask." He stroked his goatee thoughtfully. "I was in town that night, at a meeting with a prosaic concerning an investment opportunity. I'll have Anna send you his contact information so you can confirm, of course."

Swift nodded. "Thank you, that would be very helpful. Are you aware of anyone that might have wanted to kill your mother? Any recent threats?" Her face was a picture of sympathy.

He leaned back in his seat and rubbed his chin, eyes distant. "I'm sure there are dozens of people that wanted my mother staked," he said thoughtfully. He shook his head and refocused on Swift. "If there were any threats, she didn't tell me about them. After we disagreed about the path my life would take, she took every effort to distance me from her business."

"Were you aware of any rivals, despite the distance?" I asked. For the most part, it seemed better to let Swift do the talking, but we needed to press him a little. If she wanted to play good cop, I could certainly play the other side.

"There are a few major players she butted heads with, but anything I know is common knowledge," Alberto said, deflecting my question. "For the past decade I've stayed occupied with my own investments."

"When was the last time you spoke with your mother?" I asked, tapping my fingers idly against the arm of the chair. Every answer served to distance Alberto from her, which only convinced me more and more that he worked for her.

"About four days ago," he replied, resting his arms on his desk and clasping his hands together. "I had offered her an investment opportunity, something I'd hoped would show her the benefits of legal business."

"What are your businesses exactly?" I asked. "We saw quite a bit on charitable donations, but not nearly as much on profitable businesses. Was your mother funding your lifestyle?"

Alberto's jaw clenched at that comment. "Hardly. She did set up a fund for me when I was newly turned, which I leveraged to make smart investments that pay out large dividends. That isn't uncommon for supernaturals, especially vampires."

Swift watched me from the corner of her eye, but I couldn't tell if she was irritated or not. "There is one person, in particular, that we suspect might have been involved," Swift said, drawing his attention back to her. "Frank Castiglione." She lifted her tablet, showing him a picture of the mafia leader.

Alberto's eyes flicked over the photograph, but he didn't seem to react. "Is he one of my mother's colleagues? His face seems familiar, but I don't think we've ever met in person."

"We believe so, though it's not clear if he was a rival, or someone she worked with," Swift explained.

There was a brisk knock at the door and Anna poked her head in. "The Guild is on the phone concerning the cremation," she said.

Alberto nodded and stood. "Tell them I'll be just a moment, please, Anna."

"Yes, sir," she said before hurrying away.

He turned back to us. "Unfortunately, it appears I need to cut this meeting short. I hope you understand."

"Of course," Swift said kindly. We stood, and I, at least, was happy to get out of this house. "If you think of anything, or find any information in your mother's records, please give me a call," Swift said, passing her card across the desk to him.

He took the card and tucked it in the pocket of his slacks. "I'll walk you out."

We followed him out of the study and walked in silence for a moment.

"How long have you lived here?" Swift asked curiously as we walked down the hall.

"I've had this house for just over a year. It's a nice retreat from the bustle of the city, something I value more the older I get," Alberto explained. We reached the front door, and as he opened it, runes flared on the trim.

I paused, curious. "Those are unique," I said, leaning in to examine the unfamiliar shapes.

"Ah, yes," he said, his chest puffing up with pride. "I commissioned a custom security ward for my homes. I'd be happy to share the rune set with you if you'd like to have this at your apartment; I've given it to most of my friends. It's years beyond the standard security runes you can find on the market currently."

"I might contact you in a few days for that," I said with a friendly smile.

"I'll let Anna know to be expecting your call. She can get all the particulars for you," Alberto said, clapping me on the back.

We walked outside and stayed silent until we climbed into the car. Vampires had very good hearing.

Swift shut her door and turned to me. "He's more involved with his mother's business than he's letting on."

"I agree," I said, cranking the engine. "However, I still don't think he had her killed. He's too image-conscious. If he had killed her, he would have made it look natural."

Swift nodded, pursing her lips. "Let's hope Castiglione knows something. If he doesn't, then we're out of leads."

TWENTY-EIGHT

I wrinkled my nose as the smell of cigarettes hit me like a battering ram. The packed room was filled with the clink of glasses and too loud guffaws of drunks. A woman with breasts almost as big as her head walked by and winked at me. She was hot, but she was also probably a high-end escort. While I could afford that kind of thing, it had never sat right with me to pay for *that* kind of attention.

"Seriously?" Swift said.

"What?" I asked, tearing my eyes away from the view as the woman walked away.

"Exactly," she said with a smirk.

Swift turned and shoved her way up to the bar. Her dress, much as I didn't want to admit it, had exceeded expectations. It was a skin-tight little black dress with a v-neck deep enough to make my mouth go dry. But I was a professional. I'd kept my mouth shut other than to tell her she looked nice. Just to be polite.

"Vodka soda for me, and whatever he wants," she said, pointing back at me.

I raised a brow, but wasn't about to turn down a free drink. "Gin, straight," I said. The bartender nodded and quickly poured our drinks. Swift shoved cash across the grimy bar then handed me my gin.

"What's the game plan?" she asked.

"I don't have one," I said, taking a sip that burned its way down my throat. It wasn't quality gin by a long shot, but it would do. I preferred the sake from the other night with Master Hiko.

"You dragged me all the way out here, and you don't even have a plan?" Swift demanded, clenching her drink angrily.

"I find them restrictive," I said, patting her on the shoulder and striding into the crowd. This kind of place attracted a certain type of people: the desperate, the not quite middle class, and the wanna-be gangsters. The not quite middle-class types stayed toward the front. They wanted a taste of the wild side, but didn't actually want to deal with the consequences. They came here, drank cheap liquor, played poker with other people like them, and then took the stories back to run-down subdivisions.

The desperate and the gangsters could always be

found in the back. All the desperate knew how to do was lose at gambling and get farther in debt. Once they got in deep enough shit, they ended up selling drugs on street corners or laundering money.

Laughter poured out from behind a beaded curtain. A woman walked out, and I caught a glimpse of something bright on the wrist of someone leaned back in a chair. The beads fell back, obscuring my view. I took another sip of my drink and walked to the doorway.

A hand blocked me from passing through. I looked at the hand, then back up to the hulk of a man it was attached to. Judging by the unfortunate bushiness of his sideburns, I was guessing werebear. Those guys were practically unkillable, and definitely not the type I could beat in a fistfight.

"VIP section only," the werebear said, his voice gruff.

I pulled out four ten-thousand-dollar bundles of cash. "Is this VIP enough for you?"

The werebear narrowed his eyes and grabbed one. He pulled a single, hundred-dollar bill from the bundle and examined it to make sure it wasn't a fake. He nodded in satisfaction, then snapped his fingers and pointed in my direction. A woman jogged over with a wooden case of chips.

"All of it?" he asked, grabbing a handful of sleek, black chips to count out for us.

"Yeah, twenty thousand for me, and the same for the

lady," I said, gesturing at Swift. The bear handed us each a stack of forty chips. I guess they bet big here.

The bear reached back and parted the beaded curtain, waving us inside with a smirk. I stepped through, ready to see if my gamble would pay off.

TWENTY-NINE

Frank was here, but the man was not looking well. He sat at the big table that dominated the room. I'd seen him around Seattle, and in mugshots, before. He was one hundred and seventy centimeters tall with broad shoulders and an abundance of chest hair that curled out of his button up shirt. Normally, he'd have a girl on each arm, but tonight he had a half-smoked cigar and a scowl.

"You're bluffing," he said sourly, sliding two more chips into a healthy pot. I couldn't see the face of the guy Frank was playing against, but he was clearly beating the socks off Frank.

There were three other guys at the table, all Frank's men. Every single one of them had folded, leaving the battle to their boss.

The new guy wore a sleek black suit that was obviously new. It was expensive, but not custom, judging by the way it hung around his shoulders. Must be newly rich if he was wasting money on off-the-rack suits and gambling at a run-down place like this.

He had his arm wrapped around the shoulders of the woman sitting next to him. Her sleek black hair cascaded over his arm. She glanced back and looked directly at me, though no one else seemed to notice us. She wore a modern version of a kimono with a bright green pattern. I had thought Swift was beautiful when I first met her -- an impression that quickly changed -- but this woman was something else. Her delicate features were perfectly proportioned. Her kohl-lined eyes were a bright hazel, almost yellow in fact.

"Bluffing, Frankie? That's what you said last round," the guy laughed, his voice younger than I expected.

I cringed. Nobody called Frank Castiglione, Frankie. But Frank didn't explode out of his seat and sock the guy. His men only twitched a little. Something weird was going on.

Frank ground his teeth together. "Are you gonna bet or just sit here wasting my time?" he demanded, leaning back in his chair and taking a big puff of his cigar.

The kid shrugged and matched the bet. "Let's see who was bluffing," he taunted.

Frank flipped his cards over, showing a straight. It was a decent hand, especially with a table of five players.

The kid just laughed and tossed his cards down on top of the pot. He had a full house.

"Two in a row," he said, scraping the chips toward his growing pile. "What are the odds?"

Frank puffed on his cigar, his eyes narrowing. His thugs kept looking at him, waiting for the sign to act, but Frank didn't budge. "Odds are low," Frank said, his voice strangely calm.

What was he waiting on to tear this guy apart? It was obvious he was cheating. No one ever got two full houses in a row. It just didn't happen.

I slipped my hand around Swift's waist and strode forward. She resisted for a second, then realized my angle and followed along. I stopped behind the chair to the kid's left. He wasn't quite as young as his voice suggested, but he was still in his early twenties, at most. College-aged and clean-shaven. Definitely not the type you expected to see here.

"Do you have room for two more?" I asked, setting my stack of chips on the table. Swift set hers down, as well, and beamed at the men, but her smile was lost on them. They weren't looking at her face.

I couldn't help but stare at the woman next to him. Her eyes hadn't left me since we walked in the room. I needed to focus, but I could already tell that was going to be a struggle.

The kid leaned around me, checking out Swift.

"There's always room for a pretty lady," he schmoozed. I had no idea why he was looking at anyone else while the yellow-eyed woman was sitting next to him. "And I guess you can join. I don't mind taking your money too."

I pulled out Swift's chair first, then sat down. Frank squinted at me. It was possible he recognized me. We hadn't ever officially met, but he'd probably seen me around the same places I had seen him.

The woman cracked open a fresh deck of cards and shuffled them with nimble fingers. She looked at Swift and smiled. It wasn't friendly, more like she knew something Swift didn't. I leaned back in my chair and looked at Swift. She had the same expression, and I was starting to feel uncomfortable trapped between them.

"It's nice to have another woman at the table," she said, her tone implying the opposite as she quickly dealt the cards.

"I'm sure the attention gets overwhelming when it's just you," Swift replied, her voice a sickly sweet tone I had not heard out of her before.

The kid laughed loudly, looking back and forth between them, then nudged my shoulder. "Women, huh?"

I looked down where he had wrinkled the sleeve of my suit and brushed it smooth. "I'm not sure what you mean," I said, taking a sip of my drink.

The kid cleared his throat and grabbed his cards off

the table. His sleeve rode up a little revealing a diamond encrusted watch with a brand emblazoned on the face that screamed money.

Frank and the others all looked at their hands, but I left my cards on the table. Poker was a game of luck, and bluffing. Based on the uneasy look the kid was giving me, this was the right strategy. I didn't care if I won or lost, so the cards didn't matter. Considering the guy next to me was cheating – though I'm not sure how – they mattered even less.

This game was about getting information, and I could get that easier if I upset the balance of power at the table. Frank needed to win, that much was obvious. Because of that, the kid held all the power right now, but I was going to take that away from him.

Frank started the betting, throwing a chip into the center of the table. Swift was next, and she matched his bet. The kid, of course, put in four chips with a sneer. The three goons folded immediately. At this point, I had to assume they were there as muscle, not to play.

"Have we met before?" Frank asked me as he traded in two of his cards.

I shrugged and waved the play over to the kid, leaving my cards untouched on the table. "I don't think so," I said, not quite lying.

"Are you not even going to look at your cards?" the kid asked, drawing my attention away from Frank.

"Is it bothering you?" I asked, raising a brow.

The kid huffed in annoyance and traded out two cards. "I don't care what you do. It's your money, man."

The betting continued, and I took my measure of the other three players. Frank was smart, not too cautious, and not brash. Even losing this badly, he was mostly unruffled. Swift played a textbook, and boring, game of poker. She most likely had two or three of a kind; just enough to stay in the game, but nothing good enough to justify drawing the other players into a betting match. The kid just threw chips in like he was confident he'd get them back, which is a great way to make sure you get caught cheating – then get an ass beating.

The play went around the table a couple more times. Impatient, the kid dumped enough chips in on his turn to make me raise a brow. Frank shook his head, but matched the bet and looked to Swift. She folded and leaned back in her chair. I pursed my lips, then shoved in half my chips.

"Dude, you haven't even looked at your cards. Is this some kind of bluff?" the kid asked.

I took a drink before answering. "I'm just feeling lucky tonight."

The kid rolled his eyes and muttered something under his breath, as he pushed in enough chips to match my raise. "I call," he said, grabbing his cards and flipping them over without waiting for me to show mine first. It was another full house. The odds of getting that hand three times in a row are fifty thousand to one. *No one* is that lucky.

"Interesting how you keep getting those," Frank said, smoke drifting from his chapped lips.

"Poker is my game," the kid responded, anger flashing in his eyes.

I looked between them. There was some history there I didn't understand. From the expression on Frank's face, I didn't think he understood what the kid was implying, either.

I picked up my cards and flipped them over. It took a moment for the hand to register. It was a straight flush.

"What the fuck," the kid exclaimed, spreading my cards out farther to check them. "How did you do that?"

"Do what? It's just luck of the draw," I said. He was more than surprised I had beat him. He was mad.

He sat back in his chair and glared at the woman next to him. She was looking at me with a smile on her lips. Somehow, she had given me the winning hand this time. I still had no idea how they were cheating, though, or why she had gone against the instructions he had clearly given her.

"Did you not expect anyone else to be able to win a hand?" Frank asked. The threat in his voice was clear. Whatever his reasons for sitting through the game, it was clear now that he had never planned on letting the kid walk out of here with a single dollar of his money.

The kid slipped his hand into his pocket, and the woman stiffened, a flash of anger rolling over her features.

"Normally, coming into a place like this, I'd expect to lose every hand. Just seems fair for the customers to win every now and then," the kid said. The easy-going confidence was gone, replaced with anger and nerves.

"What are you implying? You think I cheat my customers?" Frank asked, flicking the ash from his cigar into the crystal ashtray at his elbow.

"Not implying, I'm stating it as a fact," the kid said, shoving his chair back as he stood. He tried to pick up his chips, but Goon Number One grabbed his wrist, squeezing hard enough for the little bones to grind together. "Let go of my hand," the kid snapped.

Frank waved the man back, and he let go. "I think we should play another round, maybe with a new dealer."

"I'm not interested. Let's go," the kid snapped at the woman. She rose to her feet stiffly.

"You're not going anywhere," Frank said. He rose, his chair sliding back loudly on the scuffed floor. "You think I would just let you and your girlfriend stroll into *my* establishment and cheat us out of all our money, just because you requested her to deal?" His anger was clear now and some of the blanks had been filed in. "You will stay and sit with a new dealer, or you can leave in a wheelchair with shattered knees."

The kid took a step back, walking right into the werebear that had greeted us at the door. Swift stood as well, though I wasn't sure whom she was planning on fighting.

Eyes darting around like a cornered animal, the kid removed his hand from his pocket. He was clutching something tightly. The woman was staring at it like she wanted to rip it out of his hands. It all clicked in my head. She was a kitsune. And this was our murderer.

"Kill them all," the kid said, looking at the kitsune, "and use him to do it." He thrust his thumb over his shoulder at the werebear.

The woman disappeared in a fiery flash. The werebear shuddered, then growled as his eyes glowed yellow.

THIRTY

I hated werebears, not in a bigoted sort of way, but in an I-hate-anything-that-can-kick-my-ass kind of way. That was the thought that flew through my mind as I was flung backward across the room. I hit the ground, and the little bit of air that was left in my lungs was forced out.

I groaned and struggled back up to a sitting position. Pink magic blazed around Swift as she traded punches with the thing. He was half-shifted, fur sprouting from his face, and two-inch claws jutting out of his broad hands. He moved like a boxer, but Swift was all fury. It was hard to fight something like that. She clocked him on the jaw, and he actually stumbled back. I was reluctantly impressed; she was doing this in heels after all. Just how strong was she?

I scanned the room for the kid, but he was long gone,

lost in the rush of screaming people all trying to squeeze out the same door. I thought about chasing him down, anyhow, but Swift took a hit from the bear that knocked her flat on her back. I wouldn't abandon my partner in a fight she was losing, even if I did want to be rid of her.

Frank pulled a worn pair of brass knuckles from his pockets and slipped them on his calloused hands. "Pull yourself together, Ringo!" he shouted at the werebear as he leaped into the fray, getting two punches in before the bear turned and swatted him away like an annoying bug. He hit a table, crushing it, and didn't move again.

I grabbed my katana, but didn't draw it. This werebear was a pain in my ass, but he was also a victim here. I couldn't just kill him; I had to subdue him somehow. Swift dragged herself back up to her feet and began summoning her mace.

"We need him alive, Swift!" I shouted. "Don't crush his head."

"That was one time," she shouted back at me with a snarl, "and I didn't know he was being possessed at the time." She leapt forward and kicked him in the back, disturbing the bear's pummeling of two of Frank's goons.

I charged in after her and kicked the bear from the opposite side. He roared in pain and swiped at me, but his attack was wide and slow. Swift jumped on his back, wrapping her mace around his throat. She squeezed, the muscles in her arms straining against the bulk of his neck. Damn, that's hot. Why does she have to be *my* partner?

Taking advantage of the distraction, I dropped to my knee and traced a rune on the ground. It glowed in a bright trail from my fingertip, the magic scorching into the wooden floor. One down, two to go.

The bear swayed forward, trying to throw Swift off his back. She held on like a rabid raccoon and began to headbutt him from behind. Did I mention Berserker Mages are crazy?

He roared and stumbled back. I darted around them and burned the second rune into the floor.

The bear dropped to his hands and knees, reached back, and threw Swift into the wall. That had to hurt. His yellow eyes turned to me. I lunged to his right and got halfway through the final rune when he hit me like a battering ram.

Unlike Swift, there was no room for me to fly back. His fist crushed me against the wall, and I could have sworn I heard a rib crack. He snarled, a gust of hot, stinky breath blowing over my face.

"Eat a Tic Tac, you oversized Winnie the Pooh," I shouted, as I got my feet under me, braced them against the wall, then pushed back with a tight grip on my katana. Mayhem magic, focused by the sword, fed power through my body. I couldn't match his strength for long, but I was not about to die in this crappy bar squished against the wall like a cockroach.

I took one step forward, then another. His boots slid back on the floor inch by inch. Swift appeared and punched him square in the eye, then kicked him between the legs. He dropped to his knees, his hands flying to his now sore fur balls.

I grabbed Swift and dragged her back, then finished the rune with two sharp lines. Each of the three runes glowed bright red, then a crackling net of pure magic surged over the bear, pinning him to the ground.

Swift wiped a line of blood away from her mouth. Her dress had ripped halfway up her thigh on the left side. "I hate werebears," she muttered.

"For once we agree," I said, pushing myself back to my feet. Everything hurt.

The bear strained at the crackling net, roaring loudly.

"Oh, shut up," Swift said. She struck him once, right behind his jaw. Her fist connected with a loud crack and the bear went limp.

"Did you kill him?" I asked, watching his chest for signs of breathing as he slowly reverted to his human form.

"No, of course not," Swift said. The Berserker rage was gone, and she was back to looking appalled that I would ever suggest she might accidentally kill a civilian.

"Is he still possessed?" I asked.

Swift leaned down and pulled his eyelid open. The faint glow was still there. "I think he is."

"We need to try to interrogate him then, and possibly exorcise the kitsune after," I said, pulling out my cell phone. "Viktor can help us if we can get the guy to the coroner's building."

"What's the point in interrogating him? Won't he just keep trying to kill us?" Swift asked.

"I don't think so," I said, thinking about everything that had happened during the game. "The kitsune doesn't want to be doing this. I think she'll find a way to help us."

"Maybe," Swift said, glaring at the bear.

I smirked and dialed the pickup service. We needed to do this as soon as possible.

THIRTY-ONE

The werebear banged around inside the transport vehicle. It was built for supernaturals; it could hold a vampire, shifter, and even a mage. I still kept a close eye on it, as the entire vehicle shook from the bear's escape attempts.

Viktor walked outside, looking pale in the sunlight. I wasn't sure I'd ever seen him outside. He preferred the company of the dead in the morgue.

The necromancer raised a brow and crossed his burly arms, straining the seams of his white lab coat. "You have brought me something still alive? I am a coroner, not a babysitter," he said, glancing at the werebear with distaste.

"He's possessed by a kitsune," I explained, glancing back at the vehicle. "But someone is controlling him. I'd like to interrogate him in one of your zombie rooms.

The only holding cells we have at the station that could contain him are closed up like that transport vehicle."

"I still don't see why this is my problem," Viktor said, tapping his finger against his chin thoughtfully. "But the necromancy containment room should hold the shifter."

Swift jogged over. "I got it," she said, holding up a to-go bag.

"How many?" I asked.

"Twenty-four. It was all they had," Swift said, handing me the bag.

I grinned at her. "That should be enough."

The werebear wrapped his meaty hands around the bars of the cell and shook them once before jerking his hands away with a pained hiss. Smoke drifted up from his palms, as the silver-infused bars had scorched his palms.

"You hungry?" I asked, shaking the bag in my hand.

The werebear paused. His nose twitched in a distinctly un-bear-like movement. "Depends on what you have," he said, suddenly calm.

"Why don't you have a seat, and I'll show you," I said, pointing at the stool in the center of the room.

The bear narrowed his eyes at me, then strode over to the chair and plopped down. I opened the bag and pulled out the first container. I cracked it open and peered inside. The perfectly shaped rice balls sat in a neat row.

The bear sniffed impatiently. "What is it?" he demanded.

I turned the container around to face him, and he licked his lips eagerly. I slammed the container shut. "I have a few questions. Each one you answer truthfully earns you a snack." In my experience, the way to a woman's heart is through food.

The bear's lip curled up in a sneer and he scoffed at me, but his eyes never strayed from the container.

"What's your name?" I asked.

"Ringo," he replied, smirking at me.

"Not the bear, whoever is in his body," I clarified. "I know you're the kitsune that has been robbing places, then killing the supernaturals you used to do it."

"Oh? Is that a fact?" the bear asked, tilting his head to the side in a feminine gesture. "Sounds pretty farfetched."

"I also know that human somehow stole your ball," I said stepping up to the bars. "How did he manage that? I thought kitsune were supposed to be the tricksters."

She snarled at my taunt. "I thought you already knew everything."

"I never said that. For example, I don't know why you let me win that last hand of poker," I said, shrugging my shoulders. “I assume he ordered you to make sure he won. How did you get around it?”

“He only said that Frank and his men had to lose,” she snapped, before a self-satisfied smile spread across the bear’s face. “He should have been more specific.” It was odd to see the burly werebear make feminine gestures.

I picked up a rice ball and tossed it through the bars. She caught it easily and popped the entire thing into the bear’s mouth, smacking her lips as she scarfed it down.

“That’s why you had him win with a full house every time, too, wasn’t it?” I asked, smiling at her. It was crafty and made his cheating obvious.

She shrugged and examined the bear’s nails. They had been chewed down to the quick. She grimaced and dropped the hand back to her lap. “I’m sure I’ll have to go soon. Why are you bothering to interrogate me, anyhow?” she asked.

“Where is the man controlling you?” I asked.

She rolled her eyes. “Never, never land,” she said in an obvious lie.

“Is he in Japan?” Swift asked, stepping up beside me. She picked up a rice ball and took a bite. The kitsune narrowed her eyes unhappily.

“Maybe,” the kitsune replied.

“What about New York, is he there?” Swift asked again.

"Maybe," the kitsune repeated.

Swift popped the rest of the rice ball in her mouth and chewed slowly. The kitsune's eyes followed the movement of her lips. Swift swallowed noisily, then leaned in toward the bars. "Is he still in Seattle?"

"No," the kitsune said with a smile.

That was smart. Once you knew she had to lie about his whereabouts, the lie became obvious.

Swift grabbed two rice balls and tossed them to her. The kitsune caught one with each hand and shoved the first in her mouth.

The bear's body twitched and the other rice ball fell to the floor. He looked up with bright yellow eyes. "He's not nearby, and he definitely won't try to kill you," she said, before falling face first onto the concrete and going still.

Viktor walked up, stretching his hand out through the bars. "The kitsune is gone," he said, turning back to face me.

"We got what we needed," I said, crossing my arms. She had told us everything she could.

"What are we going to do with all these rice balls now?" Swift asked.

THIRTY-TWO

We knew he was in Seattle. We knew that he was nearby. And we knew that he was going to try to kill us, but we still didn't know who he was. I thought of him as a kid, but he was over twenty, old enough to have graduated college. He had this look about him, though, that made me think he had grown up soft. He hadn't lived around the mobsters all his life, but he was pissed at Frank, specifically. Who could lure a young guy like that into the seedy underbelly of Seattle?

Swift stood in front of the System screen in the conference room we had taken over. She had changed out of her dress into a pair of jeans and a simple button-up shirt. I forced my eyes away from her backside and refocused on the board.

She scrolled through a series of mugshots, searching through everyone connected to Frank who had been arrested in the last year. All those men had the tired eyes of someone who had been scrambling just to get by their entire lives. This kid had looked more like the rug had been jerked out from under him and he didn't know how to handle it.

"We're getting nowhere with this," I said, leaning back in my chair and putting my feet up on the table.

"Don't put your feet up there," Swift said, frowning at me.

I pushed my feet farther onto the table. "We're looking in the wrong places," I said, smirking at her annoyed expression.

"Where should we be looking then?" she asked, crossing her arms.

"I was trying to think of what would make a clean-cut kid like that show up at a gambling den," I said, rubbing my hand against the stubble growing out on my jaw. It itched when it got to this length. I really needed to shave. "We have a college-aged guy, who most likely grew up middle class and suddenly needed money. The first victim was a well-known loan shark. We were looking at it as a strike by a rival, but what if it was something more straight-forward? What if this guy owed her money he couldn't pay?"

"He'd be able to pay her if he robbed the bank," Swift argued. "Why would he kill her?"

"Maybe she humiliated him, or hurt him or someone

he cared about," I said with a shrug. "You ever watch *21*? They were mathematical geniuses – the type smart enough to trick a kitsune, but stupid enough to get into gambling with the mob." When you gamble with the mob, the odds don't always play out like they should.

"You're thinking college dropout?" Swift asked, already swiping the mugshots away and typing the new search into the system. Names and faces popped up on the screen.

"Narrow it down to the best universities, and the most expensive. He was desperate," I said, pulling my feet off the table and walking over to join her at the board.

Swift typed in the additional parameters, then added a few more detailing his approximate age, race, and hair color. The system popped up the results. There were four hundred and fifty-two people who fit the description.

"I really thought that would narrow it down more," Swift said, scrolling through the results.

"Wait, scroll back up," I said. One of the faces had caught my eye. Swift moved the list back up, and I clicked on the one I had recognized. He was a little younger in his picture, but I had no doubt it was our guy. Chad Murray, twenty-three. He had dropped out of school one semester before graduating with a bachelor's degree in Mathematics.

"That's definitely him. I'd recognize that smug face anywhere," Swift said, pulling up all his known addresses.

"He's going to be living in someone else's house," I said, halting her search. "Actually, we should look at Frank's first."

"You're right. He is taking everything away from the people that he feels victimized him," Swift agreed. She pulled up Frank Castiglione's addresses. He had three houses in Washington. Two were in remote areas, but only one was downtown.

"Let's go," I said, grabbing my jacket from the back of my chair. "We've got a dirtbag to bury."

THIRTY-THREE

Downtown Seattle was a mix of tall buildings, hills, and pedestrians that clogged up the already narrow streets. I laid on my horn, which was as anemic as the engine, as a couple strolled into the crosswalk when I was trying to make a right turn.

"Pick up the pace, people!" I shouted out of the window.

Swift scowled at me from the passenger seat. "We should be waiting for backup."

"I'm not risking this guy getting away again," I said, speeding around the turn once the pedestrians got out of my way.

Frank lived within walking distance of Pike Place Market in some old lofts that had been there since the 1800s. The bright-red brick stood out from the grey stone buildings that rose up on either side. He had the corner penthouse with the best view of Elliott Bay. I parked in a no parking zone halfway on the curb and jumped out of the car.

We flashed our badges at the security guard, who didn't seem to care one way or the other, as we jogged inside. The building still had that old-world feel. The walls were lined with wood paneling and exposed brick. The floors still had the original, scuffed dark wood. Thankfully, the elevator was new.

I followed Swift into it and pressed the button for the top floor. We zoomed upward. Magic crackled through the air as she summoned her mace.

"This building is a historic landmark. Do not blow it up," Swift warned.

"I'll do my best," I said, as we stepped out into the hall. "But I'm more worried about the holes you might leave in it."

Swift looked extremely unimpressed. "Unlike you, I generally manage to avoid collateral damage."

As the elevator opened, a woman stepped out of the apartment next door to the penthouse. Swift held up her badge with her free hand, then pressed her lips to her fingers, silencing the woman. Her eyes went wide, and she ran for the elevator.

As we walked down the hall toward the apartment, information flooded my senses: the scent of old wood that made the whole building smell a little like the library Swift took me to the other day, Swift's slightly quickened breathing, and the quiet thump of our feet against the floor.

Another woman was arguing on the phone with someone I assumed was her boyfriend. Her hushed, aggravated tones seeped out into the hallway. The mayhem magic inside of me reveled in the anticipation of the impending confrontation.

The door to the apartment was nondescript. There was no welcome mat and no ominous sign that announced a mobster lived inside. I wondered if any of the people who lived on this floor realized that their former, and current, neighbor weren't exactly upstanding citizens.

Swift stepped to the left of the door and pressed her back against the wall. She lifted the mace up, holding the wooden handle with both hands, her knuckles white. Smoky, pink magic leaked from her eyes as she met my gaze and signaled she was ready.

I left my katana sheathed but drew a rune to create a barrier behind us. The magic sparked from my fingertip as I traced the intricate shape. As I completed it, bright lines burst from the edges of the rune, creating a cage around us and the door. No one was getting past it, especially not a human.

I wasn't sure how difficult it would be to fight the kitsune, if it came down to it; I had to ensure it couldn't escape from the room. Neither of us had said it aloud, but we both knew there was a chance the kitsune might try to possess one of us.

The door handle was cold to the touch. I was surprised when it turned without resistance. It was unlocked. Swift shifted into a crouch, and I pushed it open. The gruesome sight that met us made bile rise in the back of my throat.

I swallowed it down and continued inside without hesitation. No matter what you saw when entering a hostile situation, you couldn't stop. A mistake like that would get you killed.

Frank hung from the beams that stretched across the kitchen and dining room. His face was purple and swollen, and his vacant eyes were bright red from the capillaries that had burst as the weight of his body had caused the rope to crush his trachea. He had died slowly and painfully.

I ground my teeth together. Frank had probably done a lot of wrong in his life, but I doubted he deserved to die for his crimes. Even if he had, it should have been quick and painless. Life is shitty enough when we aren't killing each other like animals.

Swift stepped into the room first. I followed and went left toward the living room, while she went right toward an open door that appeared to lead into a bedroom. The apartment was quiet, but I couldn't shake the feeling that we weren't alone.

As I walked carefully forward, I noted that Frank had kept his house clean and neat. The kitchen had been updated to include modern appliances, but it still had that old-world feel to it.

A long table was set in front of the wall that separated the kitchen from the living room. A single chair lay on the ground; it had been tipped over with enough force the arm had broken off. Frank had either been surprised by his attackers, or put up a fight.

I edged around the wall, holding my breath. The hair on the back of my neck stood on end as a familiar, and dangerous, magical signature prickled across my skin. Sitting perfectly still on the couch was the kitsune, her long black hair cascading over her shoulder.

I could hear Swift's careful steps coming up behind me as the kitsune turned her head. Her yellow eyes met mine, and I hesitated. She looked…sad.

"Show me your hands," I demanded, one hand wrapping around the hilt of my katana. I knew she wouldn't, or couldn't comply, but I didn't want to hurt her. This wasn't her fault; she was as much of a victim as Martina Bianchi or Antonio Ricci.

"I'm disappointed," the kitsune said, not making any move to show her hands.

"Why?" I asked, dread already spreading through my gut.

"The trap was so obvious." She disappeared with a flash of bright orange flames that flew straight at me.

I jerked out of the way, and the wave of heat rushed past me. I whipped around, but it was already too late. Swift's body jerked, and when she looked up, the pink glow of her eyes flickered and faded into yellow.

THIRTY-FOUR

Swift's stern mouth softened, the corners lifting into a sultry smile. Her hips rolled as she took a step toward me, letting the mace drag on the ground behind her. The floor creaked under the weight of it. It was creepy to see Swift looking at me with *that* kind of expression. I decided that I preferred the honest glares over this fake flirtatiousness.

"Did he order you to kill us?" I asked, stepping back with my hand on the hilt of the katana.

Swift rolled her eyes, brushing her short hair away from her face. "Of course he did. He has no imagination."

Her fingers tightening on the mace was the only warning I got before the runed hunk of metal was swinging toward my face. Pulling the sheath in the opposite direction of my draw, I ripped the katana free with blinding speed and parried the strike. The clash of runed weapons sent sparks flying, and, even though I was only deflecting the blow, the force of it jarred painfully up my arm. The sound it made was deafening – Swift was *strong*.

Her mace crashed into the wall that divided the living room from the dining room, bashing through the sheetrock. Dust and splinters puffed into the air as she ripped it free, charging at me again. I skipped backward, not counter-attacking, just avoiding her offensive strikes. I wouldn't – couldn't – kill her. Either of them. I had lost one partner already; there was no way Swift was dying by my hands.

I knew she, or the kitsune, was holding back. Berserker Mages weren't as common these days, but they had been plentiful during the wars. They had been heroes on the battlefield, famed for their insane power and unstoppable rages. I had to stop this fight before the kitsune unleashed the crazy. If I didn't, there would be no way to stop them without killing Swift. She'd become a risk to everyone at that point.

I ducked under a swing of the mace and lunged forward, driving my shoulder into her stomach hard enough to lift her feet off the ground. The back of her legs hit the couch, and she toppled backward over it.

"Take back control, Swift!" I shouted as I stalked around the couch.

She stood slowly, using the mace to push herself back onto her feet. "Swift can't hear you right now," she said, baring her teeth at me like a wild animal. With a growl, she leapt forward, swung the mace over her head, and straight down.

I jumped to the side as the mace crashed into the floor where I had been standing, splintering the wooden planks. She ripped it free and swung up at a diagonal that I was barely able to avoid. The momentum carried her around, and the end of the handle caught my thigh. My leg went numb from the force of the strike and I stumbled.

With a speed I hadn't thought possible, she swung the mace back around. I got my katana between me and the head of the mace, but that couldn't protect me from the full impact of the blow. It lifted me off my feet and threw me back, jarring my insides as it hit.

I was airborne just long enough to anticipate the painful impact I knew was coming. I hit the window and it cracked but didn't shatter as runes flared around it. I wanted to kiss whatever engineer and mage had come up with runetech to make improved shatterproof glass.

The pain of the blow made my vision swim, but a blind person could have seen the mace swinging at my head. I ducked and rolled underneath. Her runed mace collided with the runed glass; a blinding light followed by a sonic boom. Every window in the room, and possibly on this floor, exploded in a shower of glass that pelted my arms and back.

Well...I guess it wasn't completely shatterproof. A cool breeze blew in through the gaping hole where the windows had been.

I flipped my katana around so that I would be hitting with the dull side and struck the backs of her thighs. She stumbled, and I followed up with a kick to her elbow, hoping to make her drop the mace. The kick pushed her back, but her grip didn't falter.

Pink magic leaked around her bright yellow eyes as she turned her gaze on me. "She's so angry," the kitsune taunted. "She keeps making all sorts of interesting threats. I don't think it would actually be possible to shove her mace up my...well, that's just impolite to even say."

"For some reason, I think she might find a way," I said with a smirk. "Where is Murray?"

"He may not be very creative, but he isn't completely incompetent. I can't tell you," the kitsune said, as she lifted the mace and adjusted her stance. She charged in, faster than the last time.

The clash of our weapons was deafening. A normal katana would have shattered, but then again, a mace that heavy couldn't be lifted by any human, or even most mages. Runes on my katana basically made it indestructible – much like her mace – and Swift's magic gave her the strength to wield such a large weapon.

She drove me back, striking with both ends of the mace from unexpected angles. Her sharp movements reminded me of sparring with Sakura, Master Hiko's wife. I had always lost those sparring matches, and this wasn't going much better.

The head of the mace clipped my arm, and I lost my grip on the katana. The metal blade clattered across the floor. I parried the next blow with the sheath and jumped for my katana, tucking into a roll. I slid past it, snatching it up off the floor and deflecting her next strike.

I couldn't stop the followup from my awkward position. The wooden handle smacked against my jaw, and blood filled my mouth as my teeth cut the inside of my cheek. Stars flashed across my vision, but I ignored that and the pain. If I stopped now, the kitsune would kill both of us.

I slashed the katana across Swift's side as I lunged forward, ducking under her arm, and came up behind her. She grunted in pain, as the blade sliced through the delicate skin of her stomach. Swift turned to face me. Her shirt was cut open, and blood seeped through the thin fabric. It wasn't a bad wound; she would heal, but guilt still burned through me.

She pressed her fingers to the wound, and lifted the

hand to her face curiously. "So you finally decided to actually fight," she commented. Pink flickered through the yellow momentarily, and her jaw clenched tightly before anger flashed across her face. "Knock me out Blackwell, what the hell are you waiting for?" she growled.

My eyes went wide. That was definitely Swift. Before I had time to analyze what had just happened, she attacked. As the mace swung at my head, the pink glow, usually contained inside of it, blazed to life. Pink flames leapt from the surface like a solar flare.

THIRTY-FIVE

The bright magic whipped around the mace, buffeting me with heat. I shoved her back, my eyes stinging from the light. The dark surface of my katana drank it in as it deflected several blows.

I wanted to beat Chad Murray's face in. Whatever his reasons for wanting these people dead, nothing justified his actions. He didn't care who he hurt as he chased after his revenge. I didn't want Swift as a partner, but I sure as hell didn't want her dead, either.

As much as I hated it, I really couldn't let this go on any longer. I'd end up dead, and so would Swift, just not by my hand. However, I wasn't going to kill her.

My katana was a focus, first and foremost. I pressed my finger against the first rune and whispered the incantation to disable the rune that held back a third of my magic. The rune flared bright green before going dark. Magic rushed through my body. I shuddered at the sensation; this was destruction in its purest form.

"This is going to hurt," I said as a wave of dark energy flowed down the already black blade.

"Good," the kitsune said with a grin.

We both charged in at the same time. She swung the mace, her teeth bared and all her muscles straining. I lifted my hand and pushed my magic outward. The mace collided with the mayhem magic surging from my palm as I caught it and cracked.

I flipped the katana over and swung it at the side of her head. She blocked with the handle of the mace, but the katana cracked that as well. The mayhem magic wrapped around the wood, seeping into it like an infection.

She dropped the mace and grabbed the katana with her bare hands, kicking me in the gut as she ripped the blade from my grip and threw it across the room. It slid toward the shattered window, stopping just inches from the edge.

The mayhem magic that had been held back by the katana surged through me. Swift balled her hand into a fist and swung at me. I parried her strike and countered with a punch to the stomach, where I had cut her previously. She hissed in pain and grabbed the back of my suit jacket, dragging me down into a knee strike that knocked all the air from my lungs… again.

The mayhem struck back, billowing out in a shockwave that threw her back like a rag doll. The walls behind her cracked, groaning under the magical assault.

The risk, always, when I used this part of my magic, was losing control. Another shockwave of dark magic pulsed out of me, rolling across the room like a flash flood.

Swift lunged out of its way, and it struck the walls. For a moment, everything was still, then the wall and part of the roof exploded outward. Dust filled the room, and debris rained down on the street below. The distant sound of screams filtered past the ringing in my ears, as I held back the rest of the chaos inside of me.

Master Hiko had taught me better than that, but I was out of practice. I had relied on the katana to hold my magic back far too much.

Swift jumped to her feet and charged me. I ducked under her initial swing and pushed forward, driving my shoulder into her gut. It was time to end this. I wrapped my arms around her waist and pushed back, lifting her slightly, then slamming her down onto the floor. She had me in her guard and wrapped her thighs around me tightly, squeezing until it became even harder to breathe.

I couldn't push up high enough to punch her, but I

managed to wedge my elbow between us. She wrapped her free hand around my tie, twisting it to cut off my air. I grabbed her hand then reared back and slammed my elbow down on her face. It pained me to do this, but there were no other options.

For a split second, the yellow eyes flickered to pink and she grinned. "Hit me like you mean it, Blackwell," she taunted before the kitsune ripped control away once more.

I hit her again, and again, but it wasn't easy to knock out a Berserker Mage. Swift was struggling with the kitsune to hold back. She was stronger than I was physically; if she hadn't been, there's no way I could have held her down like this.

My elbow smashed into her face again, breaking her nose this time. Blood gushed over her lips, and her eyes began to swell. Shit, now I just felt like an abusive asshole. Every time she looked at me after this, I'd see the tears leaking out of her bruised eyes. If we made it out of this alive, she was totally going to kick my ass for this.

Pushing aside the guilt, I took my chance and pressed my elbow into her throat, while I traced a rune into the floor near her head with my other hand. It was messy and inexact, but it was all I had time for.

I broke her guard and threw myself backward as the rune flared to life. Swift tried to follow, but bright orange lines of magic wrapped around her body and dragged her back down to the floor.

She struggled against the painful net, as the magic burned against her skin. It wouldn't leave a scar, but it was painful.

THIRTY-SIX

I stood slowly, my entire body aching. Someone banged against the front door, and I whipped around, ready to fight again; but it was Sergeants Lopez and Danner shouting to be let in.

I hurried to the door and canceled the runes that fueled the barrier keeping them out, then opened the door. Lopez was halfway to shifted, black fur edging across her face, and fire was crawling up Danner's arm from his tightly clenched fist.

"We're fine," I said, walking back to Swift's side.

They followed, but Lopez brushed past me as soon as she saw Swift still struggling under the runed net. "What the hell is going on?"

"Possessed," I said, spitting a glob of blood onto the floor. My cheek still ached from the blow I had taken earlier. “The suspect wasn’t here, just the kitsune. Not that I’m complaining, but why are you two here?”

“Swift texted us. We came as soon as I saw the message,” Lopez said, as she pulled back the shift and walked over to kneel by Swift.

The kitsune smirked at her. “Swift says you’re late.”

“That’s creepy as hell,” Lopez said, staring at Swift uncomfortably.

“You got any idea where the suspect is?” Danner asked, relaxing his posture slightly.

“Yes.” I shook my head, irritated at my own short-sightedness. The trap that led us here had been too tempting. There was one last person Chad Murray wanted to get his revenge on. Someone we had overlooked after interviewing him. I really hated it when Swift was right. “Martina Bianchi had a son, Alberto. We interrogated him, but didn’t think he was involved at the time.”

“You didn’t,” Swift hissed, her eyes flashing pink for a split second.

“*I* didn’t,” I corrected with a glare. “But Murray left this trap as a distraction. That means there is someone else involved, someone that he wanted to kill himself.”

“Why do you think it’s Bianchi’s son?” Danner asked.

“It didn’t seem like he was involved in all of this, but I recognize that,” I said, pointing at an intricate series of runes on the backside of the door. I hadn’t seen it when we entered the loft. "We saw the exact same rune set at Alberto Bianchi's house. He said it was a custom enchantment, something he had made for extra security, and that he liked to share it with friends. It's proof he knew Frank. We've been wondering who got Murray into gambling in the first place, and I think this is our answer."

"That's a hell of a leap Blackwell," Danner said, looking over the runes.

"One of the charities that Bianchi worked with was connected to the college Murray attended," I said.

"We got the test results back on that hair you found at Martina Bianchi's house. The results were inconclusive. It was definitely a female vampire, but it wasn't Martina," Lopez interjected.

"It could have been Alberto Bianchi's secretary," I said, thinking back to her long, black hair. "That would make them a lot closer than Alberto wanted us to believe."

I turned to Swift. It was a long shot, but the kitsune, or Swift, might be able to answer. "Did Alberto Bianchi know Frank Castiglione?"

The kitsune struggled briefly, but Swift ground her teeth together and managed a strained *yes*.

"That's it then. That's our connection," I said, clenching my hand into a tight fist.

Lopez shrugged. "Seems plausible. If you think this

was a distraction, then you might want to hurry. Murray could have already killed Bianchi and moved on."

"I'll go with you," Danner volunteered, surprising me. "Swift shouldn't be left alone though."

"I can stay with her," Lopez said, cutting me off before I could say I'd be the one to stay. "I'm better suited to match her strength if she manages to get loose somehow. Besides, you're already beat to hell, Logan."

I didn't like leaving her vulnerable like this, but I *needed* to stop Murray. He had made this personal.

THIRTY-SEVEN

Danner crouched in front of the door of Alberto Bianchi's townhome. It was wedged between two other homes overlooking the seawall and within walking distance of Frank's loft.

Magic extended from his fingertips, undoing the locks. The runes that secured the place had already been burned through by brute force. I wasn't sure what could do that, though I suspected it might be the kitsune. She must have let Murray in here before being ordered back to Frank's apartment to wait for us.

I entered first, as quietly as I could. Unlike Frank's loft, this place was trashed. Murray had a lot of rage pent up inside of him that he had apparently worked out on Alberto's house.

A muffled voice shouted from somewhere below us. Vampires often slept in fireproof basements, as it was the safest way to ensure they wouldn't get hit with accidental sunlight, or roasted in a house fire.

Younger vampires were completely paralyzed by the sun. They slept like the dead, hence the old myths prosaics used to believe about them. Martina Bianchi had been old enough, and strong enough, to daywalk, though it led to her demise. Her son was way too young. That left him vulnerable.

We crept further into the house, silently searching for the entrance to the underground basement. I rounded a corner and saw a sleek black shoe attached to a foot sticking out of a room.

I pointed it out to Danner, and we moved forward as one. I kept my hands on my katana, ready to draw it if there was a threat. The foot turned out to be attached to the bodyguard that had checked our badges at Bianchi's other house. His face was purple and contorted in a grimace, his mouth hanging open as though he had been gasping for breath. Dried saliva coated his chin.

I knelt and pressed two fingers to his pulse point. The body was still warm, but there was no heartbeat. A thin, broken silver chain hung out of his shirt. Something had been ripped off it, most likely a security card of some sort.

"Airborne poison," Danner whispered.

Murray must have got it in the air system somehow. Supernatural security often forgot about prosaic threats.

This place was heavily runed against magic, but a prosaic had been able to take out the guards and break in all on his own.

He had above-average intelligence, but it never failed to surprise me how vulnerable supernaturals still were when it came down to it. Even a trickster had fallen prey to his determination.

We moved to the next room, a study lined with shelves of old books. One of the bookcases stood away from the wall a little, and light filtered through the crack. Danner and I noticed it at the same time. He approached it first, then pulled it open silently.

Concrete steps led down into a narrow stairwell. A pained grunt echoed up through the opening, followed by a hissed threat.

I hurried down the steps, staying as silent as possible, but I had a feeling Murray was so focused on Alberto that he wasn't paying attention to anything else. Another pained groan made me pick up the pace. Murray wasn't just here to kill Alberto, but to make him suffer.

The stairwell led to a thick steel door, which stood open. The spartan, concrete room Alberto slept in wasn't large, but it was big enough to hold the coffin he slept in. It was runed to be fireproof and waterproof to protect him while he slept.

There were two coffins in the room. One was filled

with the messy remains of a vampire – Anna, I assumed – and blood was streaked across the open lid of the other coffin. The bitter scent of burned flesh filled my nose.

Chad Murray looked younger without his suit and the blingy watches. He looked like a kid...holding a stake over the heart of a vampire.

He leaned in close to Bianchi's face. "You deserve to suffer," Murray hissed, dragging the silver-tipped stake down the vampire's chest. Smoke drifted up from the wound as his flesh blackened and burned.

"Drop the stake and put your hands in the air!" I yelled, stepping into view. I kept one hand on my katana, but summoned a ball of flickering, green fire with my other hand. Casting anything right now would risk hurting Alberto as well, which would get me in trouble.

Murray's bloodshot eyes flicked to me, but he pressed the stake more firmly against Alberto's chest instead of dropping it. "No," he spit at me. "He deserves to die!" Murray's hand tightened on the stake, but I noticed his other hung at his side gripping a strange, glinting glass sphere. There was magic of some kind inside it, but I had no idea what.

Danner slipped into the room behind me. I felt the magic he was gathering like a storm brewing. Danner was old school; he wasn't going to give Murray much of a chance to come to his senses. Against my better judgement, I stepped in front of Danner, blocking his view of the kid.

"Blackwell, get out of my way. He's got a stake to his heart; we have to end this. You can't risk trying to talk him down," Danner hissed.

"He's a kid," I said quietly, before returning my focus to Murray. "Chad, I know you want to get back at Bianchi, but this isn't the way to do it."

Murray glared at me. "It's the only way to do it! If I don't do this, he'll walk away without being punished at all! He took everything from me, and I'm not the only one," Murray shouted, practically foaming at the mouth. "I tried reporting what he was doing to the police, and you know what they did? Nothing! And you're just like them; you're going to bury this!"

"Blackwell, move, he isn't going to listen," Danner whispered harshly.

I shook my head firmly. The only justice I could give this kid was not dropping him where he stood, despite having every reason to do so.

"Do you even know what he did? He recruited me! He took me to the gambling house himself the first time, told me I could win a lot of money instead of having to waste my time at some bullshit minimum wage job," Murray spit out. "But it was all part of the scam. Once I was so deep in debt, there would never be a way out, all because of one fucking game. He made me start figuring out new ways to rig games so he could hurt more people." Murray's hand shook with pent-up rage. "I tried to get out, but then he said he'd drain my mother if I left. I have to stop him."

Hiroji's words from the bar came back to me, taunting me with the truth. Even after all this, I wouldn't be able to arrest Bianchi. Even if I managed to scrape together some evidence on him, he'd walk in less than a day never having seen the inside of a jail cell. He was too connected, and too rich to suffer such an indignity.

Yet, the way Murray had gone about his revenge was also wrong. He had killed innocent people and had almost gotten Swift killed. To top it off, he had done it by taking away the kitsune's freedom. All of this had happened because he had been backed into a corner with no way out, and no one to help him. The IMIB should be able to protect people like him, but it didn't.

"Murray, if you kill Bianchi, I won't be able to help you at all. If you drop the stake, I will do everything in my power to make sure you receive a light sentence; but you have to cooperate now," I said, desperately trying to reason with him. I could only give him a few moments longer to surrender before I'd have to act. Waiting this long was already stupid of me, but every agent has a moment in their career when they come across someone that, despite everything, they know doesn't deserve to die.

Murray pressed the stake against Alberto's chest, digging the point in. "A light sentence?" he mocked with a hysterical laugh. "He'll have me killed! There is no way out of this, not anymore!"

I snuffed out the magic in my right hand and angled my body to hide it. With quick, practiced movements, I traced a rune into the air. Danner must have seen what I was doing because he edged around me, drawing Murray's attention. At least I hoped that was his plan.

"You dig that stake in any deeper and you won't have to worry about Bianchi, kid. I'll smoke your ass myself," Danner said. The shadows deepened around him, and he seemed to grow in size. Flames crackled up his arm and balled in his palm.

Murray lifted his left hand and shook the strange sphere at us. Danner cursed behind me, and my insides went ice cold. That little piece of glass was called a Boom Ball, which was a cute way of describing a magical grenade that would utterly destroy everything in a six-meter radius. "Come any closer, and I'll drop it!" he shouted, his hand trembling on the stake. "You wanna die protecting this asshole?"

It was all bravado. He was terrified. His only chance lay in my timing this perfectly. If I didn't, we were all about to become pink mist.

I completed the last stroke on the rune and pushed off the ground hard with my back foot, as gravity ended all around us. Murray's eyes went wide as his feet left the ground. He flailed his arms, as everyone did at the shock of gravity losing its hold on them, and the stake fell from his fingers.

So did the sphere.

I shot forward, drawing my katana with the blazing speed I had trained for so long to attain. Twisting the katana as soon as the tip cleared the sheath, I swung the blade in a wide arc and struck him in the chest with a loud thump.

The blow sent him flying into the concrete wall. His head snapped back, cracking against the unforgiving material. Blood floated up in wobbly spheres from the fresh wound.

Danner grabbed Alberto, forcing the sun-paralyzed vampire back into the coffin and slamming the lid shut.

I tucked into a flip just before hitting the wall behind the coffin and kicked off it at an angle, sending myself toward Murray.

The Boom Ball drifted through the air, pulsing red. That was the other thing about those nasty little grenades. Normally, it took a pretty hard impact to set them off, but they were also runed with a dead man's device. Five seconds after they were dropped, they'd go off, even if there was no impact. We had two seconds left.

Murray flailed frantically as I neared him. I ignored the weak hits and wrapped my arm around his neck. I kicked off the wall again and met Danner in the air.

Danner was calmer than anyone about to die had any right to be. He was tracing a shield rune into the air that wouldn't stop the blast even if he finished it in time. There was only one option left, and just like in the warehouse, it was a crappy one.

I pressed all five fingers into the runes on the handle of my katana, and released my mayhem magic in the direction of the Boom Ball. Time seemed to slow. The sphere cracked. Magic flared out of me, dark, destructive, and chaotic.

Bright orange flames burst from the sphere and billowed in every direction. The ebony magic collided with it and consumed the fire. Acting like a shield, it sent the blast in the opposite direction. But it didn't stop there.

The force of the impact threw all three of us, and the coffin, backward. My back hit the wall hard, and I saw stars.

Magic poured out of me. I could feel it like a ghostly extension of my body as it tore through the house, consuming everything in its path. It was hungry, and it was angry.

The magic reverberated with the rage I felt at Murray's situation. At the lack of justice. Maybe I should just let it go. It would destroy us. Destroy Bianchi. Destroy this city. Hiroji said I never changed anything, but I could, so easily. I could change everything.

That was why I feared my magic. It could so easily consume me, and sometimes I wanted it to. But no matter how much I hated Bianchi and everything he stood for, this wasn't the answer. Hiroji was right about me in some ways, but he was still wrong about the most important thing. It was still worth it to at least *try* to do the right thing.

Dust and debris rained down on us as the house shook down to its very foundation. The magic roared above us. I curled my hand around the katana, and, though I couldn't re-invoke the runes in my current state, I used the familiar feel of the weapon to ground me. The focus was a crutch. I didn't need it. *I didn't need it, dammit.*

With a guttural yell, I mentally clawed at the magic, dragging it back into me inch by inch. It felt impossibly heavy. Every muscle in my body strained almost to the point of snapping. My jaw ached. The pressure behind my eyes was unbearable. I kept on. Giving up wasn't an option.

The roar of destruction above us slowed, and the

dark cloud began rushing back into me. I squeezed my eyes shut, grinding my teeth together against the painful rush of energy. I was in control. Not the mayhem magic. *Me*.

With a resounding clap, the last of it snapped back into me. I fell to my knees, dropping Murray in a quivering lump on the ground.

Danner was the only one that managed to stay on his feet. He looked at me with a pale face, but a stoic expression. "What in the ever-loving fuck was that?"

THIRTY-EIGHT

Gravity came back with a vengeance, crushing us into the ground. Murray yelped like a puppy and Danner glared at me, gritting his teeth against the pressure. I quickly traced out the rune to cancel it and collapsed back against the wall.

"I've seen a lot of shit, but my previous question stands. What the fuck was that?"

My muscles trembled with exhaustion. I pushed up to one knee and looked up at Danner. "I'm a Mayhem Mage."

"You say that like it's a choice. That's a curse," he said, narrowing his eyes and chewing on a toothpick. He *had* to keep them in his cheeks. There was no other explanation.

"It's definitely not what I'd called a blessing," I agreed. Calling it a curse was something of an old mage superstition. No one really understood why a mage was afflicted with out-of-control magic, but there was always one living mage with the burden.

Murray made a sharp movement, grabbing something from his pocket. I yanked his arm up, and a small orange and yellow ball fell from his fingers, bouncing across the floor.

Before I had a chance to react, a bright flash momentarily blinded me. A fox sprinted to the ball and picked it up with its mouth. The kitsune looked at me, then vanished with a pop of flame.

The townhome had been almost completely destroyed, and the two homes on either side had been damaged, as well. Unfortunately, my magic had also hit the bridge that wound along Elliot Bay. No one was hurt, but the road was looking a little worse for wear.

It was two long hours before I made it back to Swift. Apparently, she had refused medical attention, but the medics didn't want to let her go until she could be tested for possession.

I walked through the prosaic police cars, their bright red and blue lights making my already sensitive eyes ache. Swift stood between a prosaic officer and Sergeant Lopez. She had her stubborn face on and was gesturing wildly as she argued with them.

She spotted me approaching almost immediately and pointed at me, shouting my name across the street.

"Come tell them I'm not possessed!" she demanded, her hands balled into fists and her eyes flashing.

"I don't know, you sound pretty unstable, still," I said with a grin as I walked up to the group.

"I will beat your ass *again* if you don't tell them to let me go," Swift threatened, her fingers twitching.

The officer took a step back, ready to get out of the way if she followed through on her threats. Lopez just smirked. She'd probably love to watch Swift beat me up.

I lifted my hands in surrender. "Yeah, that's definitely her talking. She's fine," I said. "Besides, the kitsune got her ball back and is free from the prosaic's influence."

Lopez turned to Swift. "Ice your face, and call me if you get any weird foxy urges," she warned, clapping her on the shoulder. "And don't forget about Friday."

"What's going on Friday?" I asked, my interest peaked.

They both glared at me. "You're not invited."

I took a step back and raised my hands. "All right. Hint taken."

"Glad to see your hair is back to normal though," Lopez said, shaking her head. "The pink was not a good look for you."

My hand flew to my head. I spun around and hurried over to the ambulance right next to us. The side mirror was at an awkward angle for looking at myself, but all I needed to see was that my black hair was, in fact, back. I smoothed my hand over it in relief. At least something had gone right today.

Bradley's voice boomed in the distance. Some poor soul was taking the brunt of his anger.

"Time to go," Swift said, hurrying over and grabbing my arm to drag me away from the crime scene. She had a slight limp, probably from my earlier strike to her leg. It didn't look like she'd let them heal her at all.

"While I'm impressed by your high pain tolerance, you do need to heal your injuries soon," I said, as I followed her into the cafe across the street.

"Yeah, I'll get to it." She grabbed a table by the window and sat down with a grimace. "I told you not to blow up this building," Swift croaked, her voice nasally because of the broken nose. Her glare was less intimidating with the bruised and bloodied face but way better at inducing a feeling of guilt.

I scratched the back of my head as I sat down in the chair across from her. "I didn't blow up the entire building," I said, staring up at the gaping hole where Frank's loft used to be.

Swift shook her head and laughed. "You know what they're calling us, right?"

"No, what?" I asked, narrowing my eyes. I had earned some unflattering nicknames in my time, so it wasn't a huge surprise to hear I had a new one.

"The Chaos Mages," she said with a grin.

I grinned right back. “It’s fitting.”

Chief Bradley’s face appeared in the cafe window, his expression thunderous. He pointed at us, then crooked his finger, demanding we join him outside. I guess a break had been too much to ask for.

THIRTY-NINE

We sat across from the Chief in his office. I was still covered in dust and grime. Swift still looked like she'd been punched in the face repeatedly.

"So, to sum it up, you destroyed the top story of a historical landmark. Then, while trying to arrest a twenty-year-old *prosaic,* you also destroyed Alberto Bianchi's home?" Chief Bradley asked with barely restrained anger.

"Well, when you say it that way, it sounds bad," I objected. "Most of the top story of those lofts are fine, it was just the one wall, and I'd like to see anyone do better while facing off against a Berserker Mage," I said, pointing at Swift accusingly.

Bradley pinched the bridge of his nose and took a dramatic, deep breath. "Do you, at least, know where the money Murray stole ended up?"

I cleared my throat, but, thankfully, Swift answered for me.

"It appears that Murray spent a few hundred thousand, but took the rest of the cash to various areas throughout the city where the homeless live, and, uh, *made it rain*," she said haltingly. "His words, not mine."

Bradley muttered something under his breath then sat up and pinned us both down with a glare. "And the kitsune?"

"Retrieved her ball during Murray's arrest and vanished," I paused, and Bradley's face darkened. "Since she was a victim in all this, we aren't making finding her a priority," I added.

Swift leaned forward. "According to Section Twelve of the Magi Treatises, the kitsune is protected under the Involuntary Acts Amendment–"

"I know," Bradley said, cutting her off. He took a deep breath. "Blackwell, pay for the damages. Swift, get your face healed, and get your expert contact to check you out and ensure you are not still possessed. I expect the two of you here bright and early Monday morning, but you *will* take the weekend off. I'll suspend you if I have to."

"Yes, sir," Swift said, sitting up like the straight-A student she probably was.

I simply nodded and pushed myself out of the chair. Everything ached. I followed Swift out of

Bradley's office, ready to head back to my apartment and relax.

"Blackwell," one of the agents said as I walked by. "A package just came in; the return address was for the kid you just arrested, so I left it on your desk."

I nodded, "Thanks."

Swift waited for me just inside our office. The package sat on the edge of my desk. It was small; whatever was inside couldn't be bigger than a book.

"Are you sure it isn't a bomb?" she asked.

"Security stamped it as safe," I said, pointing at the green symbol on the right corner. They scanned every piece of mail that came in to make sure it wasn't some kind of magical attack.

"They're not great with prosaic threats," Swift said, still suspicious.

I shrugged and pulled the top open, snapping the tape that held the lid together. Inside was a small, black notebook. I lifted it from the box, turning it over in my hands before opening it.

Inside was page after page of debts recorded by Castiglione, and the notes linked over half of them to Alberto Bianchi. This must have been what Murray took from the bank. I shut my eyes and ground my teeth together. If we had found this still in the bank, we could have used it as evidence. Murray had made it worthless simply by stealing it. It could never be used in a court case now, especially if the defendant had a competent lawyer, and Bianchi would.

"What is it?" Swift asked, sounding concerned.

I handed it to her without speaking. I was too angry to say it out loud. The same laws meant to protect the innocent sometimes protected the guilty, too. Murray was going to go to jail for years, and Alberto Bianchi, the man ultimately responsible for all of this, was going to walk. That wasn't justice.

Swift handed the ledger back to me. "Sometimes you can't get the bad guys, Blackwell."

"Is that meant to be comforting?" I snapped, gripping the notebook tightly.

"Of course not," she said exasperated. "It's just a fact. You can beat yourself up about it, or you can look for ways to change things."

I pressed my hand to the rune that locked my bottom drawer, then pulled it open. Inside were two medals I'd received in my time at the IMIB. They were shiny wastes of space. I dropped the ledger down on top of them. I wanted it there as a reminder of the cost of failure.

FORTY

I kicked the door to my apartment shut behind me, then pulled off my jacket and toed off my shoes. I couldn't track grime all over the tatami mats.

My shoulder was stiff and achy despite the healing, and I desperately needed a shower. Dust billowed out of my hair when I attempted to run my fingers through it.

Annoyed, I walked into the bathroom and turned the hot water on. Steam quickly filled the room. I stripped my shirt off and laid it on the counter, neatly folded. Despite how filthy it was, I couldn't bring myself to dump it in a pile on the floor.

I took off the rest of my clothes, folding them as well, and stepped under the spray of hot water. The dust and grime coating my skin washed down into the drain in dirty rivulets. My shoulder was purple and blue, and scrapes I didn't even know I had stung in the water. I scrubbed around the injuries then washed my hair quickly.

The hot water was relaxing. Normally, I would sit in the shower until it was like a sauna, but today all I wanted to do was sleep. I shut the water off and grabbed the towel hanging by the shower door.

My feet left wet prints as I padded out into the main area of the apartment. I rubbed the towel over my head, then wrapped it around my waist. I stepped around the shōji divider and froze. Someone was in my bed.

A fluffy orange tail tipped in white stuck up over the comforter. One of the pillows was on the floor. I stepped forward, my toes curling against the tatami mat.

There, lying on my bed, was a fox.

"What the hell are you doing here?" I asked, confused and alarmed.

The fox opened one eye and twitched her ear, then stretched her slender legs out in front of her. She rolled onto her back, nuzzling her head into my pillow and stared at me sleepily.

"Get off my bed!" I took a step forward to drag her off, but the towel started to slip and I had to catch it. She didn't budge, just burrowed further into the covers. "I mean it. Off, now."

The kitsune let out a high-pitched nasal whine, her ears flattening to her head. It was possibly the most obnoxious noise I had ever heard.

I grabbed a pair of pants, stomped back into the bathroom, pulled them on, then stomped back to my bedroom to deal with the infestation.

"How did you even get in here?" I demanded.

She huffed and rolled over to a sitting position. Magic that flickered like fire twisted up from her feet to her head, as she transformed from fox to woman. Her silky black hair was loose and a little wild, hanging around her face as if she'd just been shown a good time. She wore a white, silk kimono that slipped off her shoulders revealing the delicate line of her collarbones and the curve of her cleavage. She looked up at me from under her lashes, her full lips pushed out in a pout.

I pressed the palms of my hands into my eyes until I saw stars. On one hand, the view was great. On the other hand, just *no*. "The puppy-dog eyes are not going to get you anywhere," I said, lowering my hands and fixing her with a glare.

"That's too bad because you are stuck with me," she said, crawling toward the edge of the bed and swinging her long legs over the edge. "You saved my life and returned my ball." She lifted the orange and yellow stone from between her ample breasts. "I owe you, and therefore I cannot turn away from my duty. I must be your guardian."

My jaw fell open, and I stuttered over all the objections before settling on, "No, absolutely not."

Her eyes narrowed and she dropped the pendant, letting it swing back to her chest. "It's not optional, Blackwell."

"Why is this happening to me?" I groaned. She just sat on the bed, watching me. I turned and walked toward the kitchen. I needed caffeine to deal with this. All I had wanted was sleep. Was that really too much to ask?

The kitsune's feet hit the floor, and I heard her pad after me. She paused in the living room and sniffed the air, her nose twitching. "Do you have anything to eat?" she asked hopefully.

FORTY-ONE

"What is your name?" I demanded.

"Yui," she said, as she sat on the couch eating the last of my toast and drinking the last of my tea. A crumb fell from her lip as she chewed. She brushed it off onto the floor, and I narrowed my eyes. The kitsune was voracious, and messy.

"I've fed you, now you're going to go get a hotel room, or whatever it is you do when you aren't sleeping in my bed," I said, pointing toward the door.

Yui lifted her dainty chin and crossed her arms. "I can't be your guardian if I'm not with you. I'm staying."

"I don't need a guardian!" I shouted, my hold on my temper snapping. I was exhausted and everything still ached. All I wanted was fourteen hours of uninterrupted sleep, which wasn't going to happen with Miss High Maintenance here.

"You should get a bigger apartment," she sniffed, looking around the room, "unless you want to share a bed?" She glanced at me from the side of her light hazel eyes. Her lips turned up slightly at the edges, and the kimono barely clinging to her shoulder slipped down a little farther.

I rolled my eyes. "Absolutely not."

She pressed her hand to her mouth and giggled like some kind of virginal schoolgirl. That was really not my type. "Oh come on, you're no fun."

"And you're not staying. I don't have time to babysit you, and I can't trust a trickster. This is probably all one big lie," I snapped, the irritation getting to me once again.

"Please let me stay, Logan," she said, dropping to her knees right in front of me with big puppy-dog eyes. "I have made a vow to protect you. You saved more than my life, you saved me from–" Her eyes watered and she looked away.

For once it seemed like she was being sincere. The idea of losing my free will, of being forced to kill people I didn't even know, was awful. In some ways, it was a fate worse than death, as cliche as that sounded. Dammit, this was stupid, but my conscience wouldn't let me kick her out onto the streets. I took a step forward and patted her on the head awkwardly. "I guess you can stay, for now."

She grabbed my hips and squealed in happiness. "Thank you, Logan. You won't regret this," she beamed up at me.

"But you're sleeping on the floor."

The door opened behind me and I whipped my head around. Only one other person could just walk in like that.

"The wards let me in..." Swift's eyes went wide with shock and her lips pinched together in disgust. "What the hell are you doing?" she demanded.

I looked down and realized how bad this looked. I was shirtless with Yui on her knees in front of me, my hand on her head. I snatched it away and turned to Swift, lifting my hands in a plea. "No, that was not – she was just begging to –" Swift crossed her arms and raised a brow as if to say, go on, keep making this worse. I cut myself off and pinched the bridge of my nose. "When I showed up she was taking a nap in my bed, and now she won't leave."

Yui peeked out from behind me, pressing her cheek to my thigh. "I've made a vow to be his guardian."

I jerked my leg away like I'd been burned and fled to the couch, a safe distance from both women.

"Guardian? Good luck with that," Swift sniped, still glaring at Yui, who was glaring right back. Shaking her head in annoyance, Swift slammed the door shut behind her and shoved a file in my face. "We've got another case," she said, a glint of excitement in her eyes.

"What happened to taking the weekend off even if he had to suspend us?" I asked. Not that I minded. Sitting around my apartment all weekend, especially with an unwanted visitor, would have been hell.

"Someone stole the ashes of a phoenix."

"A phoenix? One of those hasn't been seen since the Mage Wars," I said, grabbing the file and flipping it open. The report had come in just a few hours ago. "If they manage to resurrect it..." I let the threat trail off unsaid. We both knew what would happen. And it wasn't good.

"We've got to find it. Soon. Bradley said he didn't even care what you blew up this time," Swift said with a smirk.

I pushed up to my feet. "I'm not blowing up anything this time," I said, smacking the file back on her chest.

"Is that a fact?" she taunted.

"Yes," I replied.

Yui watched eagerly, her eyes bouncing back and forth between us.

"How about a little wager then?" Swift offered. Berserker magic frothed in the depths of her dark pink eyes. Deep inside, whether she wanted to admit it or not, she was just like me. Full of chaotic, out-of-control mayhem.

"You lost the last one, which means you can't be a

total pain in my ass about the rules anymore. Are you sure you want to make another wager?" I taunted.

A muscle in Swift's jaw jumped as she ground her teeth together. "I'm sure. What about you? You're not scared, are you?"

"Loser has to house the kitsune," I said, jabbing my finger at Yui.

"Hey," Yui objected. We both ignored her.

Swift narrowed her eyes. "It's on, Blackwell."

We shook on it, those golden threads tying us together once more. I was not losing another damn wager. I was in control, and nothing was going to take that away from me.

ALEX STEELE

BLOOD OF THE COVENANT CHAPTER ONE

Fire rained down from above, streaking across the sky like fireworks. Glass shattered overhead. A man and a woman ran from the shrieking monster that loomed above the city. We were running out of time, and out of options.

I sheathed my katana and raced forward, weaving through smoldering cars and craters the size of a bus. Swift was a few meters ahead of me, her red trench coat trailing behind her like a matador's cape.

The phoenix leapt into the sky, its wings unfurling in a blaze of oranges and reds. It was *huge*. The wing tips crashed through skyscrapers, searing glass and metal with the unbearable heat. Protective runes flared but were burned through instantly.

Whoever had resurrected it wanted anarchy. They

wanted to destroy, nothing more, nothing less. A phoenix couldn't be controlled no matter how strong the mage or warlock. It was a weapon of mass destruction that would kill the summoner as soon as a random passerby.

We were not prepared for this.

I picked up my pace, jumping up onto the back of a half-crushed car, stepping my way onto the precariously leaning roof of a liquor store. Chief Bradley was supposed to have given us the weekend off, but no. He had to send us after some idiot who stole, and summoned, a phoenix. I should have been sleeping like a baby right then, not fighting for my life and the fate of New York City.

"Come and get me you ugly ass carpet bird!" Swift shouted, waving her mace like a baton. Carpet bird didn't even make sense. She must be getting tired.

The phoenix shrieked, insulted, nonetheless, and dove at Swift. She swung her mace, pink magic flaring all around her. It hit the creature square on the beak, but it didn't stop the thing. It shoved her back, crumpling the ground beneath her feet.

I took a running leap onto its back, drawing my katana as I flew through the air. I wrapped both hands around the katana and stabbed down as my feet hit slippery feathers. The blade sunk into the creature, but I could not keep my footing.

The phoenix reared back with an angry shriek. It twisted its head around, snapping at the unwanted passenger currently stabbing it in the neck.

A wing hit me, almost making me lose my grip on the katana.

"Distract it!" I shouted down to Swift.

"I'm trying!" Swift shouted back. "But you shouldn't have jumped on the back of it you idiot!"

I ground my teeth together and tried to drag myself farther up, but the bird twisted and shook. I caught a glimpse of the fury in its eye. This thing had seriously woken up on the wrong side of the nest.

A sudden burst of pink magic blazed up underneath the bird. It shrieked in pain and launched upward, twisting in the air until my feet were dangling over the city. The katana slipped once, then tore free and we both fell. I'm not saying I screamed, but the noise that came out of my throat wasn't manly.

I cast the shield rune built into the katana just in time to hit the asphalt. The magic protected me, but the sudden stop was still jarring.

I canceled the rune and climbed out of the small crater. My suit was singed. My head was pounding. And the acidic blood of the phoenix had burned my hands.

The phoenix dove at Swift. She swung her mace upward, catching it on the beak like a hook punch. I ran toward them, frantically trying to come up with another plan of attack. What we were doing wasn't even slowing it down.

I sheathed my sword. It was time to fight fire...with ice. Pulling on the magic churning inside me, I focused it, shaping it to my will. With a deep breath, I thrust my palms toward the phoenix. Bright, white magic soared toward it, hitting its vulnerable underbelly. Ice flowed over the bird, creeping along its wings and up over its face.

Swift charged in immediately, hitting its leg and knocking it off balance. The phoenix shrieked in anger, and fire erupted from its beak. The pillar of flame shot up into the sky.

The ice immediately began melting, running off the fiery, piece-of-shit pigeon like a waterfall. Swift leaped forward, but her foot slipped on a half-melted chunk of ice and she fell face first on the pavement. Her mace slid just out of reach.

I raced toward them, jumping over her just in time to deflect a blow from the phoenix's clawed foot. It flapped its wings furiously, sending ice and water everywhere, blinding me.

"Dammit, Blackwell!" Swift shouted, dodging under the wing as she tried to get back to her mace.

I sliced through a feather, but was almost sprayed with blood. "Let's see you come up with a better idea!

Just hitting it with your mace isn't actually *doing anything*," I yelled back.

I dodged left when my legs were swept out from underneath me. My back hit the pavement, and my katana clattered out of my hands. Upside down, Swift looked back, half-apologetic, half-annoyed.

"Watch where you're going!" she said, exasperated.

"How about you watch where you're swinging that thing!" I snapped, rolling through the slush to grab my sword.

The asphalt rolled under our feet. Swift looked at me, her eyes wide. This wasn't the phoenix. They could breathe fire and were apparently indestructible, but they did *not* cause earthquakes. I grabbed my sword and ran after Swift who leapt over a car to escape the sudden earthquake. This was all wrong.

Behind us, the ground split open, and green fire erupted from the crevice. It swallowed cars and a deluge of melted ice. Steam poured out like a fog as cold water hit hot air.

The phoenix fell halfway in and screamed, fire pouring from its beak. Its massive wings beat in a panic, sending debris and steam flying in every direction. Whatever was coming out of the earth was hotter than even the phoenix could stand.

Dark magic shuddered in the air all around us.

Something, or someone else, was there. "You feel that, right?" I hissed.

Swift nodded, adjusting her grip on her mace and searching the area around us. "Look out!" she shouted just as I saw a cloaked figure step into view.

Get your copy now!

CAST

Logan Blackwell – Logan Blackwell is a long-time agent at the International Magical Investigations Bureau. He is a Mayhem Mage, cursed with a rare and chaotic magic. Blackwell likes to do things his way, and is particular about his cars, suits, and food.

Lexi Swift – An eccentric Berserker Mage, and new IMIB agent. She transferred from the Magical Artifacts division and is now Logan Blackwell's partner. She wears a blood red trench coat, knee high leather boots, and has short pink hair. As a Berserker Mage, she is a formidable fighter, and a little bit crazy.

Chief Bradley – Chief of the Homicide and Robberies Division of the IMIB. A stocky and wide man known for his loud rants and keen intellect. It is suspected the tank is named after him.

Sgt. Lopez – Sergeant with the IMIB, Homicide and Robberies Division. A short woman with dark-brown hair and eyes the same color, and a round face that makes her look approachable. However, she is a determined and intelligent officer that doesn't let anyone push her around.

Viktor – Coroner at the IMIB and a necromancer. He can raise anything from the dead as long as the head is still intact. The Russian man has an imposing presence, a chiseled jaw, and is suspected to have wrestled a bear...and won.

Sgt. Danner – Sergeant with the IMIB, Homicide and Robberies Division. Looks unkempt, and lives by the motto: If it ain't my problem, it ain't my problem.

Master Hiko – An old Japanese mage and master of *battoujutsu*. He took Blackwell in after his parent's death and trained him, teaching him control, and giving him the katana that holds back the mayhem magic. He has a long braided beard which he often tucks into his belt.

Sakura – An old Japanese woman, and ninja. She also

helped raised Blackwell after his parent's death, though she refused to train him citing that he was "too full of chaos to ever learn the way of the ninja". She is scary accurate with shuriken, and often appears and disappears with no warning.

Billy – An employee at Rune Rental in Moira. Billy is in his early twenties, a little bit timid, but loyal to Blackwell. He is always trying to get Blackwell a better car after he inevitably destroys his current ride.

Professor Gresham – Owner of Gresham Rare Books. He has unruly white hair, bushy eyebrows, and thick glasses. Professor Gresham has known Lexi Swift since she was a child and is very fond of her.

Hiroji – A member of the yakuza under his father, and former best friend and childhood companion to Blackwell. Hiroji has dark black hair, a piercing gaze, and a good poker face. He carries a katana, however unlike Blackwell's, it is not used to focus his magic.

Alberto Bianchi – A vampire, and son of Martina Bianchi. Claims to not be part of the mob, but is revealed to be very deeply involved. Appears to be in his early thirties, despite being about eighty years old. A goatee hides a weak chin and ages him a little.

Chad Murray – A human that was forced to drop out of college after accumulating a large gambling debt. He tricked a kitsune and stole her ball, then used her to take revenge on the mob that wronged him, harming innocent people in the process.

Martina Bianchi – A vampire who was almost two-hundred years old before her death. She had been involved with the mob her entire life, and had a reputation as a cutthroat loan shark. She is the first victim killed after being possessed.

Antonio Ricci – A werewolf and mob enforcer. Employeed with Martina Bianchi. He is the second victim killed after being possessed.

Sgt. Patrice Jackson – An old mage who guards the records room, commonly known as "The Cave". She is sweet as Southern apple pie if treated right, and vicious as a moccasin if pissed off. She is rumored to keep the remains of a stupid individual that attempted to force their way into the records room in a jar in her drawer.

Peterson – A clumsy detective that is incapable of watching where he's going or keeping his coffee in a cup.

GLOSSARY OF PLACES & FOREIGN WORDS

Magical Revolution – Much like the Industrial Revolution, this merging of supernatural magic and human technology changed the world and spurred both races to new and exciting innovations.

Moira – A multi level city accessible only to supernaturals. The lower levels house the Rune Rail system, and the upper levels are filled with shopping, apartments, and supernatural governing bodies. No one knows how Moira was built, or where it is, other than the mages that created it.

Rune Rail – A train system that travels through a interdimensional portals, taking supernaturals in and out of the city of Moira.

The Edge – Moira is not surrounded by a wall, instead, when you reach the borders of the strange city it simply...ends. The Edge is the place where it dissipates into a strange, murky darkness. A force field prevents anyone from falling off.

Arigatou gouzaimasu – *Thank you* in Japanese. This is the first form of thank you when speaking to someone in a higher social class than you in Japan.

Arigatou Gozaimashita (ありがとうございました) – *Thank you* in Japanese, specifically for something that has happened in the past.

Battoujutsu – The art of drawing the sword. The training is for combat effectiveness through distancing, timing, and targeting. It is not practiced as a sport.

Kanpai – The Japanese word for "Cheers!" in a drinking toast.

MAKE A DIFFERENCE

Reviews are very important, and sometimes hard for an independently published author to get. A big publisher has a massive advertising budget and can send out hundreds of review copies.

I, however, am lucky to have loyal and enthusiastic readers. And I think that's much more valuable.

Leaving an honest review helps me tremendously. It shows other readers why they should give me a try.

If you've enjoyed reading this book, I would appreciate, very much, if you took the time to leave a review. Whether you write one sentence, or three paragraphs, it's equally helpful.

Thank you :)

P.S. Who's your favorite character? Let me know in the Facebook group.

https://www.facebook.com/groups/thechaosmages

AUTHOR NOTES

First, I want to say *thank you* for reading this story. It has been a joy to create. My intent for this story was to entertain, after all, life is heavy on all of us at some point.

I have always been an avid anime fan, and that was something else I wanted to bring to this series. The story was sparked from the idea of a tough-guy detective, with no desire for a partner, being matched up with an equally tough (probably tougher) female partner. I had to write it.

This is the result, and I hope to continue playing in the world I have created for a long time.

Secondly, I want to thank several authors who have been either incredibly helpful or inspirational – in many cases both.

Orlando Sanchez - Not only has he been more

helpful than I could have asked for, he was part of the inspiration for this story. When I read Montague and Strong Case Files, I could not put it down. At the time, I had been doing market research as to what genre I wanted to write in. Reading M&S gave me the inspiration for The Chaos Mages Blackwell and Swift. To Orlando if you read this ありがとうございました (Arigatou Gozaimashita).

Shayne Silvers - Nate Temple was another breath of fresh air. The Urban Fantasy genre is mostly dominated by female-led characters. And for good reason, most readers are female and the many male readers out there also enjoy reading about strong women (at least I do). Reading Nate Temple solidified for me, that there is a market for male-led or tough-guy urban fantasy. I hope that I was also able to provide some balance by forcing Blackwell to have a strong female partner.

M.D. Massie - Thanks for a great panel at the Boston Fantasy Fest on how to write fight scenes. Having over 15 years' experience myself in martial arts, I felt like an idiot after the panel. So many of the things I find basic after years of practice (read getting kicked in the head, or choked out) were left out in my writing. Things I just forgot to add because they have become instinctual to me.

Domino Finn - He a very personable and funny guy. We met at Boston Fantasy Fest, and he was gracious enough to provide some useful insight on using local myths and adding them to the story.

John P. Logsdon - His Ian Dex series was another fun read. He also helped me with ReaderLinks, which allowed me to have a smooth process for the ART (Advance Reader Team).

Michael Anderle - Last but not least. He is the founder of the 20Booksto50K group, which has been beyond helpful in becoming an author. You would almost certainly not be reading this book had it not been for his group. So, Michael, if you read this, thank you!

Alex Steele is not just one author, but two. The person who you will see on all social media under the Alex name is me, Alex. But, my wife, Stephanie Foxe, has written the bulk of the story. The story is my idea, and I give her chapter-by-chapter plot lines. She then writes it and I go back over it to make changes to give it the tone I'm after. I will put more about us in the about the author section, for now I wanted to have her say a few words, too.

From Stephanie:

First of all, thank you so much for reading this story! When Alex came to me with the concept, I was so excited to be able to help him write it. And now, I am thrilled we can share it with you. A badass detective with control issues? And a Berserker Mage with a giant hammer? Hell yes! I am so ready to blow more shit up.

We'll be diving deeper into mythology as we continue the series, and putting our own spin on the stories that entertained us for years, like DragonBall Z and Rurouni Kenshin. This series is all about fun, kicking ass, and making a meaningful difference. Basically, action with heart.

As Alex said, all of the authors listed above have been so helpful in launching this series, and our careers. Thank you, from the bottom of my heart.

Follow Me

Thank you so much for buying my book. I really hope you have enjoyed the story as much as I did writing it. Being an author is not an easy task, so your support means a lot to me. I do my best to make sure books come out error free. However, if you found any errors, please feel free to reach out to me so I can correct them!

If you loved this book, the best way to find out about new releases and updates is to join my Facebook group, The Chaos Mages. Amazon does a very poor job about notifying readers of new book releases. Joining the group can be an alternative to newsletters if you feel your inbox is getting a little crowded. Both options, and Goodreads, are linked below :)

Facebook Group:
https://www.facebook.com/groups/thechaosmages
Newsletter:
https://alexsteele.net/#Follow-Me
Goodreads:
http://goodreads.com/alexsteele

ABOUT THE AUTHOR

Alex Steele is the brainchild of husband and wife team: Alex and Stephanie. The persona you see online from Alex Steele is all Alex, but you can find his wife on social media as Stephanie Foxe.

Alex got his itch for writing after Stephanie began to write and publish her series. Previously, he'd never read books (I know crazy right?). He immersed himself in countless hours of research to better help his wife succeed. It was during that time that he began reading dozens of books and thought, "Hey maybe I can do this writing thing too." It turns out writing is hard (who knew?).

What he did learn is that he could outline stories reasonably well and that Stephanie enjoyed writing his ideas. So, Alex Steele was born: Alex comes up with the overall concept, and Stephanie writes it. Alex then reviews it and makes edits. We pass that work on to an editor, then finally to ART (Advanced Reader Team).

We hope you enjoy reading the stories as much as we enjoyed writing them.

RECOMMENDED READING BY ALEX STEELE

Witch's Bite Series by Stephanie Foxe

Montague and Strong Case Files by Orlando Sanchez

The Temple Chronicles by Shayne Silvers

The Colin McCool Series by M.D. Massey

Black Magic Outlaw by Domino Finn

The Ian Dex Series by John P. Logsdon & Christopher P. Young

The Unbelievable Mr. Brownstone by Michael Anderle

www.AlexSteele.net

facebook.com/AlexSteeleAuthorPage

goodreads.com/alexsteele

Made in the USA
Middletown, DE
14 February 2019